# SACHIE'S HERO

## BROTHERHOOD PROTECTORS HAWAII
### BOOK SEVEN

## ELLE JAMES

TWISTED PAGE INC

ISBN PRINT: 978-1-62695-656-8

*Dedicated to my lovely sister who is a complete badass in her fight against cancer. I love her so much!*

*Elle James*

# AUTHOR'S NOTE

Enjoy other military books by Elle James

## *Brotherhood Protectors Hawaii*
Kalea's Hero (#1)
Leilani's Hero (#2)
Kiana's Hero (#3)
Casey's Hero (#4)
Maliea's Hero (#5)
Emi's Hero (#6)
Sachie's Hero (#7)
Kimo's Hero (#8)
Alana's Hero (#9)
Nala's Hero (#10)
Mika's Hero (#11)

Visit ellejames.com for more titles and release dates
Join her newsletter at
https://ellejames.com/contact/

# SACHIE'S HERO

BROTHERHOOD PROTECTORS HAWAII
BOOK #7

*New York Times* & *USA Today*
Bestselling Author

**ELLE JAMES**

# CHAPTER 1

*THE TORTURED TEEN buried his face in his hands and hunched over in the chair. "I didn't want to hurt anyone."*

*Sachie's heart squeezed hard in her chest. She leaned forward and touched the young man's arm. "You don't have to hurt anyone, Luke."*

*When he'd shown up at her office as she was closing the door to leave for the day, he'd been distraught, almost what she considered manic. His hands shook, and his eyes were wide and wild.*

*She hadn't had the heart to tell him to come back in the morning. Instead, she'd let him in, ushering him into the room where they'd conducted their counseling sessions.*

*Now, he glanced up at her, his eyes filled with tears. "I'm just like my father. I'll always be like him. What choice do I have? I have his DNA; I'm hardwired like him. I can't escape it."*

*"Yes, you can," Sachie assured him. "If you stay on your*

medications, you can control the ups and downs of being bipolar. You won't be as susceptible to the mood swings. But you have to stay on the meds. They help you regulate the chemicals in your brain that are making you feel the way you do. You don't have to do it on your own."

Luke shook his head. "It was only a matter of time before something bad happened, and I lost my shit. I knew someone would get hurt, and I'll never forgive myself. It's no use. I can't have a real life. I can never trust myself with a girl. I mean, look what I did to Kylie." He waved his hand in the air. "The girl I care more about than anyone—I put her in the hospital."

Sachie's stomach clenched. "What happened, Luke?"

Again, he buried his head in his hands. "I never wanted to hurt her. She was my everything, and I hurt her!" He leaned back and stared at his hands. "I hurt the girl I love. Instead of her, I should've hurt myself." He pounded his fist into his forehead. "Why am I this way? Why can't I be normal?" He continued to pound his fist into his forehead, leaving a red mark that grew bigger with each blow.

"Luke, you can't beat yourself up." Sachie reached out to capture his wrist in her hand, halting his assault on himself.

He jerked his hand out of her grasp and leaped to his feet.

Sachie backed away several steps, giving herself distance from the tall, gangly teen. During their sessions, he'd never hit her, but hadn't he just admitted to putting his girlfriend in the hospital?

*He paced away from her. "Whatever gene it is causing me to be this way needs to stop here." Luke spun and faced her, his cheeks red enough to match the patch on his forehead. "I could never have a kid of my own, knowing I could pass this down to him. I wouldn't wish this mental disease on anyone. It's genetic, I tell you. I don't want to end up like my father, in jail for murdering my wife. He killed my mother in one of his rages. That's how he ended up in prison. That's how I ended up in foster care." He pivoted on his heel and faced the wall. A print of a Hawaiian beach with stately palm trees hung in front of him, a scene meant to instill a sense of serenity.*

*He swept his hand across the print, knocking it off its hook. The picture landed with a crash on the floor, the frame shattering into pieces.*

*Sachie fought to remain calm, though her heart hammered against her ribs. She eyed the door, gauging the number of steps it would take to reach it should she need to make a quick escape. The problem was that she'd have to pass near the teen on her way out. He'd hurt his girlfriend. He might hurt Sachie.*

*He turned to face her, his brow furrowed, deep shadows beneath his eyes as if he hadn't slept in days. "Everything was going better than it ever had. I was in school, doing my community service at the Honolulu Boys' Club after school, and I saw Kylie in the evenings and on weekends. I even liked working with the younger kids." He grimaced. "I almost believed I could have a real life. I could be differ-*

5

ent." He snorted and strode past Sachie to stand, staring out the window.

The view from the window was of a garden filled with colorful bougainvillea, a stark contrast to the teen's dark and dangerous mood.

Sachie took another step backward, edging toward the door while Luke's back was to her. She hated feeling defensive. Her job was to help this young man, not run from him. She couldn't bail on him like so many others had. But damn. Her receptionist had left before her. Sachie was alone, with no one to help her if Luke turned violent toward her. She sucked in a breath and let it out slowly. Panicking wouldn't help her or Luke. "Did something happen at school that set you off?"

The young man shook his head, rocking back and forth, his hands rubbing against his thighs in nervous thrusts.

"Did something happen at the Boys' Club?" Sachie persisted.

Luke stopped rocking and stiffened.

Had she struck a nerve?

His fingers curled into fists.

"Something happened there," Sachie stated. "You were angry when you left to meet Kylie."

"I wasn't angry with her," Luke said as if pushing the words through clenched teeth.

"Talk to me," Sachie urged. "Tell me what happened. Maybe I can help you sort through your feelings. We can *go through the techniques I showed you to help you manage your anger."*

*He pounded his fist into the window, cracking the glass.*

*Sachie jumped, emitting a startled yelp.*

*"Didn't you hear me?" he yelled, staring down at his bloody fist. "I'll never be able to manage my anger. I'm damaged. You can't fix me."*

*"Luke, the medicine helps—if you stay on it. You can't just quit taking the medication. You need it to allow you to live that normal life you want. You can have the marriage, children and a career if you stay on the drugs that regulate the serotonin in your brain."*

*"That's just it." He spun toward her. "I got into drugs because I felt like I had multiple personalities. There was me, and then there was the other me. The other me couldn't control his moods. When I got caught with the drugs, I was ordered into rehab to get off the drugs."*

*"And you did," Sachie reminded him. "You've been clean for months."*

*"And yet, you tell me I have to be on drugs to get the voices in my head to stop making me crazy?" His brow twisted. "Trade one drug for another? No. I can't live like that. The way I see it, I'm one missed pill away from killing someone."*

*"You aren't going to kill anyone," Sachie said. In all her sessions with the young man, she'd never felt threatened or afraid. Until now. "Self-medicating with cocaine wasn't the answer."*

*He gave a bark of laughter. "That's the one thing I can agree with. It was hard to let go of the mind-numbing effects of cocaine. It was so damned hard. I don't wish that shit on anyone. And I never want to be involved in helping others...what did you call it?" His eyes narrowed. "Self-medicate. I kicked it, but not everyone can. I really thought I'd won that battle and never had to go back there again."*

*"And you don't have to go back," Sachie tried to reassure him.*

*"I can't. I won't. It makes me angry all over just thinking about it. No matter what happens to me, I will never go back to that life, even if it means losing everything and leaving me with the voices in my head."*

*Sachie frowned. "Did someone at the Boys' Club try to give you drugs?"*

*Luke's gaze avoided hers. "Kylie didn't understand. All she wanted to do was help me. I couldn't let her. She wouldn't listen."*

*"So you hit her?" Sachie whispered the question.*

*Tears welled in Luke's eyes. "I didn't mean to hurt her. I was trying to stop her. If she'd done what she was going to do..." His voice trailed off as his fist clenched, causing more blood to ooze from the cuts sustained from the cracked window.*

*Sachie fought back the urge to run from the room and call 911. "Luke, did you hit her?"*

*He continued as if in a trance, his voice monotone, his gaze on the bleeding hand. "When I grabbed her arm, she jerked away and fell, hitting her head against the corner of* the building." He stared at the thick red drops now falling to the floor. "There was so much blood..."

"You said you put her in the hospital." Sachie needed to know Kylie was getting medical attention. "How did she get there?"

Luke raised his head, looking directly at Sachie but not connecting, as if he was looking at an image burned into his mind. "I took her to the emergency room."

Sachie hated to ask but had to, "Was she breathing?"

Luke nodded. "I made sure they got her into an exam room. Once I knew she was in good hands, I left. She won't have to worry. I'll never hurt her again."

"Oh, Luke," Sachie moved closer and touched his arm. "You didn't hurt her on purpose. It was an accident."

"No." He shrugged off her hand. "I can't do this anymore. If I can't trust myself, why should anyone else?"

"Luke, you came to me for help," Sachie said. "Let me help you."

"There's no help for someone like me."

"There is help for people like you, Luke." Sachie stood still, wanting to take another step toward him but knowing it might make him feel like he was backed into a corner. She was losing him. "You need medication that targets the specific chemicals in your brain, not street drugs. And you need to take the medicine every day for the rest of your life."

Luke jammed his hands into his pockets. "It doesn't matter," he said, his voice flat, defeated. "Kylie will never take me back. Her parents will file a restraining order to *keep me from seeing her if they don't send me to jail. And I don't blame them. I wouldn't let my daughter see me ever again. Not after what I did to her."* He turned back to Sachie, his shoulders drooping. *"I don't need the drugs, and I won't be coming back to see you. Take me off your calendar and fill the appointment time with someone you can help."*

Her stomach clenched. *"Luke, you have to keep coming to me. The judge ordered you to see me once a week for six months. If you don't, I have to report that you skipped out."*

Luke wasn't a bad kid. He was mentally ill. The medication he'd been taking would help him where so many other mentally ill people didn't have that option. *"Take your meds. You'll be better."* She waved a hand toward him. *"You were good for the three months you were on it regularly, weren't you?"*

He nodded. *"But it doesn't matter anymore. I've blown it with Kylie. Hell, I nearly killed her. They probably won't let me go back to the school. I'm done with all of this."* He gave her a grave look and turned to glance out the window. *"Thanks for trying."*

*"You wouldn't have come to me if you didn't want help,"* Sachie said. *"Please, let me help you."*

With his back to her, he shook his head. *"I didn't come for help. You've been good to me, and I knew you would listen to what I had to say. The only help I need is for you to deliver a message to Kylie."*

*"You didn't hurt her intentionally, Luke,"* Sachie insisted. *"You should deliver the message yourself."*

*"No. Her parents will send the police to find me. I don't have much time." He turned to Sachie. "Tell Kylie that I'm sorry for dragging her into my shitty life and that I'm sorry for hurting her. She might think I'm selfish and not thinking about her, but this is the only way I can be certain I'll never hurt another living soul."*

*His voice was so emotionless, faraway and haunting.*

*Sachie's heart pinched hard in her chest. "Luke, tell her yourself."*

*"Ms. Jones, please, promise me you'll tell her all that and that I loved her more than life itself."*

*"But—"*

*"Please," he said, his voice choking on what sounded like a sob.*

*Sachie's heart broke at the sound. "I promise. But what are you going to—"*

*Before she could finish her sentence, Luke pulled a gun from his pocket. "I'm sorry," he said.*

*Stunned, Sachie didn't have time to react before the teen pressed the barrel against his temple and pulled the trigger.*

*Bang!*


"No!" Sachie Moore yelled and sat up straight in her bed. Drenched in sweat, her heart racing, it took her several seconds to realize she wasn't in her office back on Oahu.

Moonlight streamed through the window, casting

11

a silvery-blue patch of light across her bedroom floor. This had been the first night since she'd moved to the Big Island that she hadn't left the light on in the bathroom. She'd purposely left the curtains pulled back for just enough natural light from the moon and stars to chase away the darkness she'd feared since that fateful day when her patient, Luke Brown, had stood three feet away from her and shot himself in the head.

The dream had been so real. She glanced down at the pale blue oversized T-shirt she'd worn as a nightgown, looking for the blood that had splattered all over her hair, face and the white button-down blouse she'd been wearing that day in her office.

No dark droplets stained her T-shirt. She raised a shaking hand to her face to brush away the droplets that weren't there.

"Just a dream," she murmured, the soft sound of her voice echoing loudly in the silent room.

Though she had to go to work in a few hours, she knew she wouldn't be able to go back to sleep. Not when she risked sliding right back into the same nightmare that had plagued her for the past few weeks.

To say she'd been traumatized would have been an understatement. She'd canceled all appointments for a week and had walked around her apartment in a daze, going through the motions. Sachie hadn't wanted to close her eyes for fear of reliving the nightmare.

The overwhelming feeling of having failed her patient had left her gutted. Failure, nightmares and lack of sleep made her drunk with exhaustion. She'd become paranoid and suspected she was hallucinating a stalker. After a week, she'd tried to go back to work only to lock herself in her office and cancel the second week of appointments. How could she counsel others when she couldn't help herself?

At the end of the second week of being afraid of a stalker that never seemed to fully materialize, Sachie was a wreck. She'd begun to think Luke's ghost had come back to haunt her. When her friend Kalea had suggested she come to the Big Island to regroup, she'd closed her office in Honolulu, packed two suitcases with only the essentials and moved to the Big Island. Permanently.

Sachie hoped the change would give her peace and a chance to start over without the daily reminders of her failure. And maybe, just maybe, her ghost stalker would disappear completely.

Her heart still racing, Sashie threw back the sheet and swung her legs over the side of the bed. In the muted light from the stars outside, she padded barefoot to the little cottage's compact kitchen and grabbed a bottle of orange juice from the refrigerator. After twisting off the top, she debated getting a glass out of the cabinet, shrugged and turned the bottle up, taking a long drink of citrusy freshness. As she lowered the bottle, a movement out of the corner of her eye made her turn toward the window at the side of the house.

A dark, familiar face stared at her through the glass.

Sachie screamed.

The bottle of orange juice slipped from her fingers and crashed to the floor. The glass exploded, sending shards of glass and juice in every direction.

When cold juice splashed against her feet and ankles, Sachie darted a glance downward.

In the single second when she'd looked down and back up, the face in the window had disappeared.

"No. No. No," she murmured. "This is not happening. It wasn't real."

Afraid to move for fear of cutting her bare feet on the broken glass, Sachie hiked her bottom up onto the counter and scooted across the surface to the far end, closest to the bedroom. When she was fairly certain she'd gotten past the remnants of glass, she eased to the floor and ran into the bedroom. Quickly pulling on a pair of tennis shoes, she ran back through the kitchen, pausing only long enough to snatch a butcher knife from the drawer.

Armed and ready to face her tormentor, she twisted the deadbolt, flung open the door and ran out into the night, coming to a halt beside the SUV Kalea had loaned her until she could sell hers back on Oahu and purchase another on the Big Island. Tired of being scared. Tired of reliving the same nightmare and ready to face whatever it was, she stood with the knife held in front of her, straining to see into the darkest shadows.

Nothing moved, not even the usual night breeze. Birds were smart and asleep. Even the chickens that ran free over the island weren't awake yet. The clatter of the night insects was eerily silent.

Standing in the starlight, dressed in a baggy T-shirt and tennis shoes, holding a butcher knife like a crazed killer, Sachie wanted to scream her frustration.

With houses close on either side of the cottage, she didn't dare let loose on that scream, proving to her neighbors and herself she was losing her mind. No. She'd have to admit the traumatic incident had done more than splatter blood on her skin and clothes. It had left a lasting impression on her psyche, causing her to hallucinate.

She lowered her arm to her side, careful not to cut her thigh with the butcher knife.

As she turned toward the house, starlight glinted off the SUV's windshield in a strange pattern, making Sachie pause to focus on what didn't look right.

Then she realized the windshield was shattered as if something big had slammed into the glass. She looked up, half-expecting to see a palm tree hanging over the vehicle. The stars shined down from a clear indigo sky. Not a palm tree or anything else hung over the SUV.

Sachie's heart skipped several beats, and she tensed. She raised the hand holding the butcher knife and glanced around, searching for any sign of movement. A shiver of apprehension snaked down her spine. Moving slowly at first, she backed toward the cottage, knees bent, ready to fight or run.

She backed in through the front door. Once she cleared the opening, she slammed the door shut, threw the bolt home and ran for her cell phone.

Juggling the butcher knife as she fumbled one-handed with the cell phone, she called the first person she could think of.

The other end of the call rang four times. Meanwhile, Sachie hurried into the bedroom, opened the closet door and stepped in.

Sachie's nerves stretched so tightly that she almost dropped the cell phone as she closed the door behind her.

Just when she thought she'd have to face her stalker alone, a groggy voice answered, "Sachie? Is that you?"

"Kalea," she whispered the only thing she could think of saying, "I'm scared."

"Why? What's wrong?" Kalea demanded, all grogginess gone from her tone.

Sachie cupped her hand around her mouth and

spoke softly into the receiver, "You know how I thought I was imagining a stalker?"

"Holy hell, Sachie, did you see him?" Kalea asked. "Are you okay?"

"I did see someone in the window," Sachie said. "At least, I think I did."

"What do you mean you think you did?"

"There was a face," Sachie said. "Then it was gone. I went outside—" Sachie started.

"Please tell me you did *not* go outside," Kalea demanded.

"Then I won't." Sachie swallowed hard and added, "But I did."

"Holy hell," Kalea said. "Are you somewhere safe?"

"I'm in the cottage. The door's locked." Sachie gave a humorless laugh. "I thought it was all in my head until I looked at the SUV you loaned me. The front windshield is shattered, like someone hit it hard. I figure if he could do that much damage to automobile safety glass, home windows wouldn't be that hard to breach." Sachie's voice faded, and her hand shook as she hunkered down on the closet floor.

"Sit tight, Sachie," Kalea said. "Hawk is on his cell phone as we speak." She paused. "I'll tell her," she said as if speaking to Hawk, and then to Sachie, she said, "Hawk called 911. They're sending a unit your way. He also has one of his Brotherhood Protectors on his way. Since he's in Hilo, he shouldn't be more than five minutes. He might even get there before the Hawaii Police Department. But don't go anywhere. Since I can't get there as fast from here on the Parkman Ranch, I need you to stay on the phone with me until the cavalry arrives."

Sachie forced a laugh. "Oh, believe me, someone would have to pry my phone out of my cold, dead hands to end this call."

"That's not even remotely funny," Kalea said.

Sachie didn't think so, either.

As she hid in the bottom of a closet barely big enough to hold her, she jumped at the muffled sound of something hitting the outside of her house, hoping it wasn't the stalker trying to get in.

She held her knife in front of her and prayed for the man Hawk had sent her way.

*Please hurry!*

## CHAPTER 2

TELLER OSGOOD JAMMED his feet into his running shoes without untying or retying. His cell phone, on speaker, lay beside him on the bed. "Did anyone call 911?"

"I notified them before I called you," Hawk said. "I sent you a pin location of the house where Sachie lives. She's only been there a little over a week." An incoming text pinged Teller's cell phone.

Teller grabbed the phone and stood, stomping his foot to set it firmly in the shoe. "Where did she come from before landing in Hilo," he asked, pulling a black T-shirt out of a drawer.

"Honolulu," Hawk said. "She left there after a traumatic incident. I don't know all the details, but Kalea said it was bad. Maybe you can get her to open up about it."

Great. Now, he was supposed to be her therapist?

"Is she working on the Big Island?" Teller asked.

"Yes," Hawk answered. "She's a teen counselor, helping with abuse and addiction."

Teller cringed. Was he supposed to dig into the counselor's psyche to figure out what was wrong? Hell, maybe he was the right man for that job. He'd been on the other side of a counselor's couch after being taken from his abusive father and placed in foster care at the awkward age of ten.

He pulled the T-shirt over his head, grabbed his phone and raced for his apartment door, glancing down at the watch on his wrist. He'd gone from a dead sleep to fully alert in less than a minute.

He looked down as he leaped past the last couple of steps from his apartment building, arriving at his vehicle in three long strides across the parking lot. Teller opened the door to the sleek black SUV and jumped in, still amazed at his find. He'd purchased the vehicle secondhand from an older man who'd lived on the Big Island but was moving to the mainland to be closer to his children as he grew older.

The SUV was in mint condition, lovingly cared for, with low miles and more than enough engine to satisfy Teller's need for speed.

Having backed into his parking space, he slammed the shift into drive and hit the accelerator hard. The SUV leaped forward. The built-in Bluetooth capability picked up the pinpoint on the map

Hawk had sent and displayed it on the screen. Teller slowed at the corner, glanced at the map to get his bearings and then made a sharp right, hitting the accelerator again. At two-thirty in the morning, traffic was almost nonexistent. Still, he remained alert, knowing those folks on the road had probably shut down a local bar and were either headed home or to the closest all-night diner, half drunk and more than half-asleep.

Teller zigzagged through the streets of Hilo, lined with houses that appeared to be straight out of an advertisement for houses designed and built in the nineteen-fifties, sixties or seventies. Each house sported a low roofline and stood close to the other like a crowd of spectators watching the parade of cars passing by on the streets.

Traveling faster than the posted speed limit, Teller wove in and out of turns and dodged cars parked next to curbs. A cat stepped off the curb onto the pavement, paused and stared at Teller's oncoming headlights.

Before Teller could hit the break, the animal spun and darted back in the direction from which it had come as if the cat had changed its mind. The result was saving Teller from making a decision to go around the beast, possibly coming to the wrong conclusion as to which direction the cat would go. He wasn't much of a cat person, but he didn't like hurting animals if he could help it.

Four minutes had passed since he'd received the call from Hawk. He realized the phone call had come to him minutes, if not seconds, from the moment when Sachie had spotted the face in the window and subsequently discovered her car had been vandalized. The perpetrator could still be at her cottage. She was lucky she hadn't been hurt at the point she'd made the call.

He still couldn't believe she'd trotted her happy ass out of her cottage to confront the owner of the face in the window.

If he was to be her protector for the next few days, weeks or whatever timeframe he was needed, he'd have to set a few ground rules. First, if he wasn't available, she should never leave the safety of her home, where she had the benefit of a lock on her door and her cell phone to call for help. Two, always assume the worst. In this case, she should have assumed what she saw was real, not a hallucination. She was lucky that the man who'd smashed the windshield on her car hadn't taken whatever heavy, blunt instrument he'd used to deliver the damage to her car and turned on her, using that instrument to crush her skull.

Teller didn't normally judge a person before he met her, but this lady appeared to fit into the category of too stupid to live. Which meant he would have his hands full if he was to protect her from a determined stalker who'd been following her around in Honolulu as well as on the Big Island.

The map guidance indicated he had reached her street, so Teller turned onto a long, quiet street, immediately accelerating. Her home was one of the last three houses at the end of the block. As he neared the pin's location, Teller slowed quickly, coming to a halt just short of a little cottage.

No strobing lights greeted him, and no other vehicles had parked in front of Ms. Moore's house. He'd arrived before the first responders.

Grabbing his Sig Sauer P365 handgun from the console, he shoved open his SUV door.

In the distance, sirens wailed, the sound growing steadily louder as the emergency vehicles got closer.

He could wait for them to arrive before he approached Sachie's home. Having backup was always a good idea, but what if the perpetrator had breached a window or door and was inside with Ms. Moore now?

No. He couldn't wait. He had to make sure she was okay. In certain situations, seconds counted.

He quickly eased up the steps onto the front porch and approached the door. When he reached for the door handle, he noticed the door wasn't closed. It stood just barely ajar, the wooden door-frame split as if someone had hit it hard.

Immediately, Teller moved to the side of the door and listened. No sounds filtered through the gap.

With the barrel of his gun, he nudged the door wider, testing the water.

Bullets didn't fly in his direction. He considered it a good sign but wasn't taking any chances. Inhaling a quick breath, he lunged through the door, threw himself into a somersault and came up into a crouched position in a shadow behind an armchair.

Footsteps rang out in the back of the house, moving quickly.

Teller's entrance into the home hadn't gone unnoticed.

A door hinge creaked somewhere near the rear of the structure, followed by the loud bang of a door slamming with enough force to shake the entire house.

The attacker was getting away.

Teller lunged to his feet and gave chase, running through the living room to a hallway that led into a kitchen. Starlight shone through the window set into the back door. He approached the door at an angle to avoid giving the perpetrator a clear target.

Gripping the door handle, he twisted it and swung it open and away from him.

Two sharp popping sounds pierced the night, followed by the dull thwack of something impacting the sheetrock on the wall across from the open door. It let Teller know the man was armed and had fired two rounds from what sounded like a small-caliber pistol. If it was equipped with a full magazine, he could have any number of bullets remaining.

He waited a moment longer. When no more shots were fired, Teller ducked low and peered around the doorframe. A tall, lanky shadow of a man was just disappearing through a hedge of bushes at the rear of the property.

Teller took a split second to debate whether to follow the man or to stay in the house and find the woman he'd been sent to protect. If the attacker had found her before Teller did, he could already have hurt or killed her. With the sirens growing ever louder, Teller turned back into the house, determined to find the woman and make sure she wasn't bleeding out. His time in the military had taught him the skills necessary to treat battlefield wounds. He knew how to stop or slow the flow of blood at least long enough for the emergency medical technicians to arrive and take over.

Not knowing whether there was only one attacker, Teller eased through the house, tiptoeing quietly and clearing each room he passed, one at a time. Hesitant to call out her name, he performed his search in silence. If she was being held at gunpoint by a second attacker, he might be willing to use her as a human shield to buy his freedom.

The kitchen was empty, the small pantry barely large enough for the narrow row of shelves, a broom and a mop. Teller checked behind a bifold door to find a washer and dryer and no additional room to hide a child, much less a full-grown woman.

He worked his way back to the hall and pushed open the first doorway on his right, finding a small bedroom barely big enough for a twin-sized bed. Dropping to the floor, he used the flashlight on his cell phone to scan beneath the bed. Nothing but dust bunnies and an old suitcase. The closet was completely empty but for a few wire hangers pushed to one side on the rod. Moving quickly, he left the bedroom and hurried to the next door along the hallway.

The second room was as small as the first, with a double bed, just the mattress and bedframe beneath. No sheets, blankets or curtains on the window. The closet was as empty as the bedroom.

After only a cursory glance, he moved to the bathroom across the hall. With his back against the wall, he nudged the shower curtain to one side. No psycho killer lurked behind it, nor was a scared woman hiding there.

He stepped out into the hallway, his muscles tensing as he studied the entrance to the only unchecked room in the corridor. The door stood slightly ajar, the doorframe splintered much like the front door.

Senses on alert, he nudged the door wider and stepped through, avoiding the pale square of starlight cast through the window. Dropping to his haunches, he peered beneath the bed. Relying on the little bit of light from the window, he discovered two suitcases, no dust and a pair of house slippers. The only door in the room had to open to either a closet or a bathroom.

He rose and padded softly across the room, setting his feet down one at a time as quietly as he could. If the woman was being held captive by a man in the closet, Teller couldn't risk making a rash move that might cause the man to react brutally, killing Ms. Moore.

If Ms. Moore lay on the other side of the door, mortally wounded, he was wasting time he could use to save her. Standing to the side of the door, he reached for the handle.

As his fingers touched the cool metal knob, the door exploded outward. A blond-haired woman burst from inside, screaming like a banshee straight from hell, wielding a wickedly large butcher knife.

Teller ducked his head and shoulders to the side, narrowly missing the blade that glinted in the starlight.

With a lightning-quick sweep of his arm, he knocked the hand holding the knife hard enough to send it flying across the room.

No sooner had the knife left the banshee's hand than the woman hunkered over and rammed her shoulder into his midsection, moving him backward like a linebacker bulldozing a quarterback.

"Whoa, hold on a minute." He staggered out into the hallway before he regained his balance. "I'm here—"

He didn't get the rest of his sentence out before she balled her fist and jabbed toward his gut.

Teller captured her small fist in his big hand but didn't twist his body around in time to avoid the knee she slammed into his groin.

"Oomph," he grunted as pain shot through him, the force of her assault taking his breath away. He doubled over, losing his grip on her fist.

The woman spun and raced away from him, heading for the back of the house.

"Wait," he wheezed, still bent over, pain radiating from his crotch through the rest of his body, making it nearly impossible for him to straighten. He gritted his teeth, fought past the pain and limped after her, struggling to get air from his lungs past his vocal cords. Finally, he yelped, "Ms. Moore!"

It was too late. She'd bolted out the back door and down from the porch.

Teller increased his speed until he sprinted after her, calling out her name. "Ms. Moore! Wait."

She kept running, crying out, "Help me! Please, help me!"

He had to stop her. Though the police cars neared, her attacker might still be lurking in the shadows of the bushes, armed and willing to shoot.

As Ms. Moore passed a concrete bird, Teller

caught up with her. He grabbed her around the waist with one arm, bringing her to an abrupt halt.

She fought, kicking and screaming.

Teller struggled to maintain his hold on her and his gun while her bare heels battered his shins.

When he turned toward the house, the woman planted her feet against the concrete birdbath and pushed hard, sending him flying backward.

He tripped over a garden paver and fell with her still clutched in his arm. He landed flat on his back, the wind knocked from his lungs. Though he lay stunned, his arm didn't loosen its hold on the squirming woman.

"Let me go!" she cried, elbowing him in the ribs. "Help! Someone, please help!"

*"That's. What. I'm. Trying. To. Do,"* he said through gritted teeth. Maintaining his hold around her waist, he rolled over, squashing her small frame between his big body and the ground.

"Get off me," she murmured, her voice strangled by the weight of his body crushing her into the grass.

"I am not the man who attacked you. I'm not here to hurt you," he said, easing some of his weight off her.

"Then why did you smash my car and then break into my house?"

"That wasn't me. Your front door was already broken when I arrived." He didn't want to move until he knew she wouldn't try to run again. If the assailant returned, Teller's body might be the only shield protecting her from gunfire. "Jace Hawkins and his wife, Kalea, sent me."

All the fight went out of her. She lay still, her breathing coming in shallow gasps.

He realized he was crushing her, but he didn't want to let her up until he was certain she wouldn't run into the attacker's range.

"The man who broke into your house has a gun. We need to get back inside before he uses it on us," he said softly. "Can you make it back to the house?"

"Only if you let me up," she grunted.

Sirens screamed loudly. Teller figured the police were on her street by now and would arrive outside her home in seconds. The perpetrator would have to be insane to stick around. Teller wasn't taking any chances. "On three, we're both getting up at the same time. Stay low and move in front of me. Don't stop, don't look back, just keep going until you're all the way inside and in the hallway. Do you understand?"

She nodded.

"Ready?" he whispered. "One...two...three." Teller pushed to his feet, grabbed her around the waist, yanked her upright and shoved her in front of him. Hunkering down, they ran toward the house.

By then, the sirens were so loud he barely heard the pop of small-caliber gunfire. Something stung his left shoulder. He didn't stop to investigate but ran faster, knowing he hadn't been stung by a bee. "Go! Go! Go!" he said, urging Ms. Moore to pick up her pace. When the woman stumbled going up the back steps, he lifted her off her feet and carried her through the open back door, through the kitchen and into the hallway, out of the gunman's range. Out of the man's range, only if he didn't follow them into the house.

Strobing lights flashed through the front windows. The police had arrived.

Teller remained in the hallway with Sachie Moore, his body bent over hers, shielding her from behind in case the attacker came through the back door.

The police stormed through the front door, spread out in the living room, one heading toward where they lay low in the hallway.

"Drop your weapon," the young officer yelled.

"I'd rather lay it down." Moving very slowly and deliberately, Teller laid his gun on the floor and slid it across the floor toward the officer.

The policeman kicked the gun behind him. "Now, raise your hands in the air and step away from the woman."

Teller straightened, raising his hands in the air, wincing at the stab of pain in his left shoulder. "The attacker went out the back. He's armed. If you hurry, you might catch him. He's already fired three rounds."

The young police officer kept his weapon trained on Teller. "I said move away from the woman."

Teller stepped backward, keeping his body between Ms. Moore and the back of the house. "The longer you wait, the further away he'll get."

"How do I know you're not the attacker?" the young officer said. "No one's leaving until backup arrives."

Another siren wailed toward them, dying down as the police car came to a stop in front of the cottage. Two more officers entered the house, all aiming their weapons at Teller.

"I'm not the attacker," Teller said. "Ms. Moore's friend sent me."

"Are you hurt, Ms. Moore?" the officer's partner asked. "Can you move toward me?"

The woman's body shook so much that her voice trembled when she answered. "I'm not hurt." She struggled to her feet and moved toward the officer. Once she made it past the officer who'd been holding his weapon aimed at Teller from the start, his partner moved forward.

"Hands against the wall," he said. "Spread your feet."

Teller wasn't going to argue with armed men who might spook and start shooting. Having been shot once that evening, he didn't want to risk taking another bullet from well-intentioned, if nervous, young officers. He turned and planted his palms flat against the wall and spread his feet wide. The fact that he could still move his arm with minimal pain was a good sign. The bullet had only grazed him. It was just a flesh wound.

The man holding him at gunpoint called out over his shoulder to the two officers who'd just joined them. "He said there's another armed assailant who left through the rear of the building. We've got this one. Go!"

Teller shook his head as the two men ran past him, down the hallway and through the kitchen. The gunman would be long gone by now.

The officer approached him, kicking Teller's heels out wider, then proceeded to frisk him, starting at his shoulders and working his way downward. When he reached his hips, he removed Teller's wallet from his back pocket, slid it into his front breast pocket and continued. When he reached the bottom of Teller's right leg, he stopped and jerked the denim up, revealing the Ka-Bar knife he kept as backup. The policeman yanked the Velcro loose and tossed the knife in its sheath toward his partner. After running his hands over Teller's other leg, he finally stood and flipped open the wallet he'd confiscated. "Driver's license says this is Teller Osgood. If this is, in fact, his wallet."

"That's my face on the driver's license and my military ID," Teller said, still leaning against the wall.

"While you're holding me at gunpoint, the real bad guy is getting away."

"We got a call saying this woman and this house was under attack. On our way here, we got another call stating neighbors heard gunshots and a woman screaming. Since you were the only one with a gun when we arrived, we have to assume you're the attacker. By rights, we need to haul you into the station and sort things out from there."

"They heard gunshots because the attacker fired three rounds."

"Those rounds could have come from your gun," the man holding his wallet said.

"Check my gun. It hasn't been fired." Teller straightened and faced the officers. He couldn't protect this woman if they hauled him into their station to *sort things out*. "Check the kitchen. You'll find two bullets lodged into the wall. Small caliber rounds, not nine-millimeter. And I didn't shoot myself in the arm." He turned just enough to point at the wound on his left shoulder, which had gone unnoticed when the officer had frisked him.

"Speaking of which," the man holding him at gunpoint said, "Does he have a license to carry?"

His partner dug through Teller's wallet and pulled out a card. "Apparently, he is licensed to carry." He turned to the woman behind him. "Do you know this man?"

Standing barefooted, dressed in nothing but an

oversized T-shirt, the woman had wrapped her arms around her middle. She shivered, though it wasn't that cold in the home. "No, I don't know him," she said, her voice trembling along with her body.

The officer pointing his gun at Teller sent him a narrow-eyed glare. "Officer Jacobs, cuff him."

Jacobs unclipped his cuffs from his service belt and approached Teller.

Teller's fighting instincts roared to the surface. It took every ounce of control inside to beat it back. The situation was bad enough with a stalker on the loose. Being led away to the police station made things even worse. Yet, punching a cop would only land him in jail. Then, who would protect the blonde who looked more like a homeless kid than a young woman? Alone, Sachie Moore would be exposed and vulnerable to the next attack. He had to work through this obstacle legally and get back to the job he'd been sent to do.

"I don't know him," Ms. Moore repeated, her voice more controlled this time, "but he took a bullet that was probably meant for me." She squinted at the nametag on the officer's shirt. "Officer...Layne, Mr. Osgood got me out of the backyard and into the house safely. This man saved my life."

Officer Layne's gaze never left Teller. He didn't say anything for several seconds and finally said, "Well, until we figure this out, he's coming with us to the station."

"What about Ms. Moore?" Teller demanded. "I was sent here to protect her."

"Tell your story to the chief," Layne said. "Ms. Moore is welcome to come with us or follow us to the station and make her statement."

Jacobs snapped the cuffs on Teller's wrist, pulled his arms behind him and cuffed the other wrist. He hooked a hand around Teller's arm and led him toward the front door, passing the woman.

"Ms. Moore, you need to come with us," Teller said. "You can't stay here alone."

Her eyes were wide. She looked more like a child in the well-worn T-shirt, her bare knees green with grass stains.

The two officers who'd gone in search of the assailant appeared in the doorway.

The first man through the door said, "We didn't find anyone, but we did find a couple of casings." He held up a plastic bag with two brass bullet casings.

As Teller had suspected—they were a smaller caliber than his Sig Sauer's nine-millimeter rounds.

"And we just heard from the chief," the officer continued and turned to Teller. "Are you Teller Osgood?"

Officer Jacobs held up Teller's wallet. "He is."

Teller nodded.

A frown passed over the officer's face. "The chief got a call from his buddy, John Parkman of Parkman Ranch."

Officer Layne frowned and adjusted his hold on his weapon. "Yeah, so?"

"You know Parkman has a security agency operating on his ranch called the Brotherhood Protectors." The officer tipped his chin toward Teller. "Parkman said they sent one of the Brotherhood here to provide protection for Sachie Moore." He turned to the blond woman. "Is that you?"

Ms. Moore nodded. "My friend, Kalea, John Parkman's daughter, is married to the man in charge of the Brotherhood Protectors here in Hawaii. I called her when I first realized someone was outside my house and that he'd smashed the windshield of my car. She said they were sending someone over to protect me." Her gaze shifted to Teller.

"That would be me," Teller said, his lips twisting. "I didn't have a chance to formally introduce myself."

Ms. Moore bit her bottom lip. "I'm sorry. I thought you were the stalker."

The man with the bullet casings nodded toward Officer Jacobs. "You can release him. He's legit."

"At least escort him out of the house before you do," Officer Layne said. "Then Ms. Moore can decide whether or not she wants him to stay."

Officer Jacobs grimaced apologetically and led Teller out of the house into the yard, where strobing lights blinded him.

"Ms. Moore, I can't protect you if I'm not with

you," Teller said as Jacobs unlocked the cuffs and freed his wrists.

Officer Layne stood with the woman on the porch, looking down at Teller. "Ms. Moore, it's your call. Do you want him to stay or leave?"

"Look, Ms. Moore," Teller said, "I could leave, go back to my apartment and sleep. You were attacked, not me. How well will you sleep without protection?"

She met and held Teller's gaze for a long moment. Finally, she nodded. "I want you to stay."

# CHAPTER 3

THE POLICE STAYED until they'd thoroughly searched her house and around her damaged car for any evidence they could find to identify the culprit.

They'd asked her to stand out of the way out on the porch.

Sachie frowned. "Okay, but first, I'd like to get dressed in something...more substantial. Could I go to my bedroom long enough to do that?"

Officer Layne nodded.

"I'm going with Ms. Moore," Teller Osgood said and moved up to stand beside her.

Her cheeks heated. "I think I'm capable of finding my way to my own room."

"Yes, ma'am," he said. "But I'd like to clear the room before you go in, just in case your attacker circled around and re-entered the house while no one was looking."

Officer Layne snorted. "With police officers all over this property? He'd have to be insane."

Osgood met and held the officer's gaze, his jaw firm. "Either I clear the room, or one of you officers can."

Layne shook his head. "Go ahead. Just don't disturb any evidence."

When Sachie stepped past the man, he caught her arm in a loose grip, his touch sending a surprise jolt of electricity through her.

She stared down at his hand on her arm, then up into moss-green eyes, a little dazed and confused. Probably from everything that had happened. "Right. You go first."

He led the way into the cottage.

Sachie followed, studying the man while he wasn't looking.

The man was tall, with a headful of dark brown hair and shoulders so broad he could be a weightlifter or a star in one of those superhero movies. A trim waist led to firm buttocks encased in dark jeans. As a protector, the man had missed his calling. He definitely should have auditioned for a superhero movie. He had the build and carried himself like one.

She stood outside her bedroom while he made a quick sweep of the closet, under the bed and behind the door. When he finished, he gave her a nod. "It's all yours, ma'am."

Sachie frowned. "Don't call me, ma'am. It makes me feel old."

"Yes, ma'am," he said, stood back and waved her into the room.

"Sachie," she corrected. "Call me Sachie."

"Yes, ma'am—"

She glared at him.

"Sachie," he corrected, his lips twitching on the corners.

The hint of a smile made her heart race. To cover her reaction, she assumed her best formal voice, the one she reserved for reporters and society snobs. "Is my room cleared to your satisfaction, Mr. Osgood?"

"Teller," he said. "And yes. You can go in. Just stay away from the windows."

"Thank you, Mr. Osgood," she said as she walked past him.

"Call me Teller," he said. "Mr. Osgood was my father."

Sachie hid a smile as she entered her room, and he left, pulling the door closed behind him.

Alone for the first time since she'd erupted from her closet, ready to stab her attacker with a butcher knife, she shivered, the events of the night rushing back at her like a tsunami of images in her mind, crushing the air from her lungs. Her heart beat so fast it burned inside her chest, and she couldn't breathe.

As a counselor, she knew she wasn't suffocating.

If she passed out, her autonomic nervous system would kick in to keep her heart beating and restore her lungs to their usual efficiency. It was just a panic attack, just like all the panic attacks she'd had since that horrible afternoon in her office back in Honolulu.

No matter how many times she'd told herself she wasn't going to die, she couldn't reason her way out of the rush of terror. She found that when she was afflicted with such an attack, if she got out of room, house or building she was in, out into the open air, she could breathe better.

Sachie ran to her dresser and pulled out a bra. As she hurried for the closet, she dragged off the T-shirt she usually slept in, put on her bra and grabbed a button-down blouse from a hanger. She slipped her arms into the blouse and left it hanging open as she tugged a pair of jeans up over her hips, buttoned and zipped. While she buttoned her blouse, she shoved her feet in a pair of running shoes and headed for the door, her chest tight, her head light as if she'd held her breath the entire two minutes she'd been in the room.

She flung open the door and raced into the hallway, slamming face-first into a solid wall.

Hands gripped her elbows, steadying her. "What's wrong?" a deep voice asked.

Sachie looked up into Teller Osgood's green eyes,

unable to catch her breath. "Out," she managed to push the word past constricted vocal cords.

"Are you okay?" Teller asked.

She shook her head, broke free of his grasp and ran for the front door.

Footsteps sounded behind her, but Sachie didn't slow until she burst through the door into the front yard.

Teller came up behind her and rested a hand against her back. He leaned close and whispered, "Breathe."

Outside in the cooler night air, with the wide-open sky full of stars shining down on her, Sachie drew a deep breath and let it out a little at a time.

"Another," Teller urged.

She inhaled again, her heartbeat already slowing.

Officer Layne looked over from where he stood beside her damaged car. "Everything all right, Ms. Moore?"

Sachie nodded, unable to respond in words. She raised her arms and laced her hands behind her head as if that would help her to better fill her lungs.

"Panic attack?" Teller asked softly.

She nodded, hating to admit to her weakness. She was a counselor, for heaven's sake. Her arms fell to her sides. Would she ever get past this? Would her life ever return to normal?

"Walk it off," Teller said.

When she didn't move, he took her hand. "It's okay. I'll be with you." In silence, he led her across the short distance of her front yard and back for several laps.

By the time Officer Layne approached her, Sachie's pulse and breathing had returned to normal. When she tried to pull her hand out of Teller's, his fingers tightened slightly, not enough she couldn't free it, but enough to make her realize she didn't want to let go. For whatever reason, this stranger grounded her when her mind spiraled uncontrollably.

"Ms. Moore, I can take your statement now, or you can come by the station later in the morning and give it," Layne said.

"I'd rather get it over with now," she said.

He nodded and pulled a pen and pad from his pocket. "You said you saw a face of a person in your window. Could you describe that face?"

The panic she'd felt moments before swelled inside her.

Teller's hand tightened around hers, and the swelling subsided.

Sachie drew a deep breath, closed her eyes and forced her mind to review the memory. "It was dark," she said. "I only got an impression of dark hair and a thin face." She shrugged, unwilling to tell them what had been nagging at her since the face had appeared. The face had been familiar, but she couldn't quite put a finger on who it reminded her of. Or her mind didn't want her to figure it out.

Layne asked her a barrage of other questions that all seemed to run together in her exhausted brain. She answered as best she could. She hadn't seen the man in the window bust her car windshield, and she'd been hiding in her closet when he'd broken through her front door and the door to her bedroom. "I'm not much help, am I?"

"You did the right thing by hiding and calling for help," Officer Layne said and turned to Teller with some of the same questions.

Sachie listened to the deep, smooth tone of his voice as he described the assailant.

"I didn't get a look at his face as he was running away from me. He was tallish, lanky and his hair was a little shaggy, not too long, but like he'd missed a haircut or two."

Officer Layne wrote down Sachie's and Teller's contact information. "We'll be in touch with whatever information we discover about this case. In the meantime, you'll need to get that doorframe repaired, and you might consider installing a security system."

The gray light of dawn crept across the sky as the Hawaii Police officers drove away from Sachie's cottage, leaving her standing on the front porch with Teller and no idea what to do next.

Teller turned to her. "If you want to sleep, I can stand watch."

She laughed, the sound a bit on the hysterical side. "I'm tired, but I couldn't sleep if I tried."

"How about I make you a cup of coffee?" he said. "I could use one."

"Why don't I make *you* a cup of coffee?" she said, leading the way back into the cottage. "That way, I can stay busy."

"Sounds good," he said as he followed her to the kitchen at the back of the house. "And maybe we can figure out who followed you here."

She stopped so suddenly he ran into her.

Her cheeks heated, and her hands clenched at her sides, her body tensing. "What do you know?"

"Only that you moved to the Big Island to get away from a stalker on Oahu after suffering from a traumatic incident." He touched her arm. "Look, you can tell me as much or as little as you feel comfortable with. The more I know, the better I can anticipate trouble. But I get it. I'm a stranger. It's hard to spill your guts with someone you've just met." He nudged her elbow. "Let's start with coffee. If all we talk about is what's the best brand of coffee, that's enough. I'm here until you don't need me anymore. Now. Breathe."

Sachie drew in a deep breath and continued into the kitchen. After cleaning up the broken glass and spilled juice, she went through the routine of filling the coffeemaker with water, scooping the dark crystals into a filter and turning the machine on. As the air filled with the rich aroma, she set two mugs on the counter, finally turning to face the stranger leaning against the counter in her kitchen. "Cream and sugar?"

He shook his head. "Black." His green eyes studied her as if he could see every thought flitting through her head.

"I like milk and sugar in my coffee." Sachie spun toward the refrigerator, yanked it open and grabbed the jug of milk from inside the door. When she returned to the coffeemaker, it had quit dripping. She yanked the pot out, sloshing hot coffee over her hand.

"Damn!" she muttered and shoved the pot back into the machine.

Teller was beside her in a second. He took the hand she'd burned with the hot liquid, led her to the sink and ran cold water over the burn.

All the while, he held her hand, and her pulse raced, her stomach fluttered and thoughts spun in her head. If she just moved away from him, she could rein all that confusion in and get her head on straight.

But she didn't move away. She let him hold her hand, trying not to like it so much. She had enough problems; she didn't need to add hero worship to them.

So, he was easy on the eye. Really easy on the eye. Sachie had dated good-looking guys before. They tended to be more into themselves than the person seated across the table. Besides, she wasn't looking to start anything with anyone, especially not with a man hired to protect her. And not while she was still suffering classic PTSD symptoms that, on many occasions, literally brought her to her knees.

As a counselor versed in all manners of trauma, she knew it took time to work through PTSD. Some didn't ever get over it. They just learned how to live with it and got on with life as best they could.

With a stalker bent on making her life hell, she didn't have time to seek the help of a therapist, so the trauma would continue. Her first goal needed to be to stop the stalker.

Teller turned off the water, grabbed the dishtowel draped over the oven door handle and gently patted her skin dry. "Better?" he asked.

She nodded, unable to say anything coherent with him standing so close and her breathing once again erratic.

"You sit." He released her hand and turned her toward the kitchen table. "I'll bring the coffee."

Sachie crossed the short distance to the table and sank onto one of the seats. "I'm not usually so clumsy," she murmured.

"And I imagine you're not used to having your home broken into." He cast a smiling glance over his shoulder toward her.

"No, I'm not." She propped her chin on her fist

and watched as Teller, who stood half-turned to her, poured coffee into the two mugs. "You live here in Hilo?"

"I have an apartment in town." Teller faced her with the two steaming mugs in his hands. He carried them to the table and set one in front of her and the other across the table from where she sat. As soon as he'd deposited the cups, he returned to the counter for the milk. "Sugar?"

"In the cabinet over the coffeemaker," she said.

He found the sugar and brought it, the milk and a spoon to the table.

While Teller sipped his black coffee, Sachie doctored hers with the milk and sugar, stirring longer than necessary as an awkward silence stretched between them.

"So, let me understand," she said, needing to fill the vacuum, "Hawk sent you to protect me. How does that work?"

He set his mug on the table. "Where you go, I go until the stalker is caught."

She frowned. "What if it takes weeks?"

Teller shrugged. "Then I'm with you for weeks."

Her frown deepened. "'With me,' what does that mean?"

"I need to be where I can see you twenty-four-seven."

Sachie raised her eyebrows. "You don't intend to stay in my house, do you? Let's be clear: I have no intention of sleeping with you or you sleeping in the same room with me. And there's no way you're going into the bathroom with me."

"Sleeping with me is not part of my job description." His lips quirked. "It's completely optional. As for following you into the bathroom, as long as I clear it first, you'll have your privacy."

"And what about my work? I counsel minors. I can't have you in the room while working with a patient. It violates client-patient confidentiality."

"You can see your patients privately...after I've searched them for weapons."

Sachie's eyes widened. "You can't treat them like criminals. They come to me for help, not to be harassed. And I'm not sure I want you to stay in my house. This is my space where I come for peace."

Teller's gaze went to the holes in the wall where the police officers had dug the bullets out of the sheetrock. "How's that working for you?"

His words hit her in the chest and sank to the bottom of her belly.

"If I'm to protect you, I must be close enough to do my job effectively." He leaned toward her. "Like I was in the backyard."

"Oh my God. I completely forgot." Sachie leaped to her feet. "You were shot. Shouldn't we be taking you to the hospital or something?"

He shrugged. "I'd forgotten about it. It can't be all that bad. It doesn't hurt much, and I have a full range of motion." He lifted his left arm over his head and winced. "It just stings a little."

"Let me see." Sachie rounded the table and stood behind him.

His dark T-shirt practically hid the fact he had blood all over his shoulder.

Sachie plucked at the fabric, trying to catch a glimpse of the wound beneath, but the shirt was glued to his shoulder in dried blood. "I have a first aid kit in the pantry. Can you get out of that shirt?"

He pulled the hem out of the waistband of his jeans and dragged it up his torso and over his head. The blood sticking his shirt to his back stopped him with his hands in the air.

"Wait," she said. "Let me ease it off so you don't—"

He gave the shirt a sharp jerk, freeing his shoulder of the shirt and the caked blood.

"—start bleeding again," Sachie finished, her words fading as she dove for the pantry and her first aid kit. She plunked it on the table and ran to her dishtowel drawer for a clean towel and washcloth. Quickly soaking the cloth under the sink faucet, she returned to Teller as a long line of blood dripped down his arm.

He twisted in his seat and held out his hand. "I can take care of it."

She raised her eyebrows in challenge. "Do you have eyes in the back of your head?"

He grinned. "No, ma'am."

"Sachie," she corrected. "Ma'am—"

"—makes you feel old."

"Right. Now, turn around and let me clean the wound. You might need stitches."

"I'm fine," he insisted.

"I'll be the judge of that," she shot back as she pressed the damp washcloth to his shoulder and gently washed away the fresh blood along with the dried. Once the wound was clean, she studied it carefully and quickly before blood started flowing again. "You're in luck. The bullet nicked you rather than embedding in the muscle.

"Like I said...flesh wound. No need for a three-hour wait in the ER to be told the same." He turned his T-shirt around from inside out and started to put it back on.

"Just a minute, Mr. Osgood. You'll need a bandage on that wound. It's still bleeding."

"Teller," he corrected. "And it wouldn't have started bleeding again if I hadn't taken off my shirt."

"Your shirt isn't a bandage," she muttered, picking through the kit to find a bandage the right size to cover the wound. "And you need some antibiotic ointment on it."

"It's really not necessary." He raised the shirt over his head.

"Seriously, you're going to argue about this?" She snatched his shirt from his hands and tossed it onto the counter out of his reach. "Now, be still until I'm finished. If you're a good boy, I'll give you a sucker."

Teller chuckled. "Yes, ma'am."

Sachie snorted. "Call me Sachie."

"Only if you call me Teller."

"I will if you quit arguing over dumb shit," she said and slathered ointment over the injury.

"It's a deal," he said and added, "Sachie."

"Better." She peeled the paper away from a bandage and stretched it across the wound and ointment. "And you're all fixed up, Teller."

He rose from his chair and held out his hand. "Thank you, Dr. Moore. Now, if I could have my shirt..."

She frowned. "Let me see if I have another T-shirt that doesn't have a bullet hole and blood on it."

"I kind of like my T-shirt. Don't you think it makes me look like a badass?" He grinned and reached around her for the garment.

"Oh no, you don't. A T-shirt is the least I can offer you after you saved my life." She shifted to block him, managing to bump into his bare chest in the process.

He caught her elbows to steady her.

Sachie's breath stalled in her lungs as she realized her hands rested against the solid wall of muscles. Her pulse quickened, and heat rushed up her neck into her cheeks. "Uh, well..." she stammered. "I'll just be a minute." She backed out of his grasp, turned and ran toward her bedroom. "Don't touch that old T-shirt!"

His chuckle followed her from the room and gave her a warm feeling all the way down the hall. All the arguing and banter had made her forget, for a few moments, that her house had been broken into and someone had almost killed them.

As she entered her bedroom, she had to pass the split wood of the doorframe, and the gravity of what could have happened hit her square in the chest. She ran to her dresser and pulled out the biggest T-shirt she could find, another she used as a nightgown that normally swamped her and came down just shy of her knees. She laughed at the faded image of a hula dancers on the front. Oh, well, it was a shirt and the biggest one she had.

While in the room, she grabbed a suitcase from beneath the bed and shoved enough clothes for a couple of days, including her toiletries and shoes. She hadn't been sleeping well with the nightmares of what had happened in Honolulu. Sleep would be impossible in the house, knowing someone had been able to break in and had almost made it to her.

She shivered, zipped the suitcase and rolled it out of the room with the hula girl T-shirt slung over her shoulder.

Sun streamed through the windows in all its early-morning glory, and a rooster crowed nearby. Teller stood at the back door, peering out at the yard, his broad, naked shoulders nearly as wide as the doorframe.

She left the suitcase in the hallway. "Hard to think that such a pretty garden is where a man tried to kill us, isn't it?" she said as she crossed the floor to him.

He continued to stare out at the yard. "It always amazes me that no matter what crazy and horrible things happen, nature keeps going. The sun comes up, birds sing."

Outside, the rooster crowed again.

Sachie smiled. "Or, in this case, the rooster crows."

"And the flowers keep blooming."

She came to stand beside him and glanced out the window, seeing what he was seeing. A yard filled with the lush tropical plants and flowers that flourished on the island. "I'd like to take credit for the abundance of bougainvillea and hibiscus, but they were there when I moved in a week ago." She held out the T-shirt. "Sorry about the hula dancer, but it's the biggest T-shirt I have."

He took the offering. "It's okay. I'll wear it proudly."

"I also packed a bag. I can't stay here."

He nodded. "I get it. Your home has been violated. You don't feel safe even with me here."

She nodded. "No offense."

"None taken." He pulled on the T-shirt, and the fabric that fit like a tent on Sachie stretched tightly over Teller's muscular frame. "If we can swing by my apartment sometime today, I can grab a shirt of my own."

"We can manage that. Especially since you'll have to drive me." Her lips twisted. "Which reminds me. I'll need to call someone to replace the windshield and repair the doors."

Teller held up his cell phone. "I had a text from Kalea. She said not to worry about the car. She has someone lined up to come by this morning to take care of it." He slipped the phone into his pocket.

"I feel bad." Sachie turned to look out at the garden. "Instead of escaping the problems I had on Oahu, I brought them with me. Now, it's impacting the people who've helped me most. And you took a bullet that was meant for me." She waved her hand toward his shoulder. "You could've died."

"But I didn't. And I'm glad I was here to help." Teller's voice softened. "You didn't pull the trigger. It's not your fault."

"Then why do I feel like it is?" Her thoughts flashed back to her office in Honolulu. To the one she couldn't help. She'd failed him.

The sound of a cell phone ringing pulled Sachie out of her pity party.

Teller patted his pocket, pulled out his cell phone and shook his head. "Not mine."

She glanced around the room, looking for the source.

"It's not in this room," Teller said.

Then Sachie remembered she'd laid her cell phone on the floor of the closet before she'd burst out to attack her intruder. She hurried back to her bedroom. By the time she found her cell phone where it had slid behind a pair of shoes, it had stopped ringing.

She checked her missed calls and didn't recognize the number. "Spam call," she said and lowered her hand.

A beep sounded, indicating whoever had called had left a voice message.

Pressing the number to hear the message, Sachie half-listened, fully expecting the caller to be someone trying to sell her a timeshare or siding for a house she didn't own.

"Ms. Moore," a familiar male voice said into her ear. In a flash, she was back in her office, standing in front of a tall, gangly, troubled seventeen-year-old.

Sachie stopped breathing, and her blood ran cold.

"You failed me," he said. "Now, you must pay."

# CHAPTER 4

S<small>ACHIE'S FACE</small> blanched a moment before her cell phone slipped from her hand. As her knees buckled, Teller reached out and pulled her into his arms.

She fell against him, her fingers digging into his shirt—her shirt—holding on as if she clung to a ledge, her feet dangling over a four-thousand-foot drop.

"No," she said, her mouth pressed to his chest, her breath warm through the fabric of the shirt. "He's dead. I saw him. He's dead."

"Sachie," Teller said into her ear as he wrapped his arm around her, holding her close. "Who was it? What did he say? Who's dead?"

"No. It can't be." Her forehead pressed into him, tipping side to side. "It's not him. He's dead."

"Who's dead?" Teller asked. "Sachie, talk to me."

Her shoulders shook with silent sobs. Deep gut-wrenching sobs that wracked her slim body.

Teller's heart squeezed tightly in his chest. He didn't know what to do. She wasn't making sense. "Who was on the phone?" he asked again.

"No. It wasn't him. It's not possible. I was there."

He leaned back long enough to scoop her cell phone from the floor and then pulled her back into his embrace. "Shhh, sweetheart. It's okay. Everything's going to be okay."

"How can it be okay?" she whispered. "I saw him die."

"Who did you see die?" he asked.

More silent sobs shook her body.

Holding her with one hand, he pressed "replay" on the only voice message on her cell phone and listened to the message.

*Ms. Moore. You failed me. Now, you must pay.*

"What the hell?" Teller stared down at the screen. In place of the usual phone number were the words Unknown Caller. "Sachie," Teller said softly, leaning back a little to look down at her. "You know the caller?"

She pressed her cheek to his chest, her fingers clenching the shirt. "It can't be."

"Who can't it be?"

"I failed him," she whispered. "Then I watched him die."

Frustrated by her answers, he tipped her chin up,

urging her to look into his eyes. "Talk to me, Sachie. Who did you watch die?"

She stared up into his face, her eyes red-rimmed. "I knew he was in trouble. I didn't stop him in time. It's all my fault. I failed him," she said, tears spilling down her cheeks.

The more she sobbed, the faster she breathed. Teller could see in her face and the way she tensed that she was sliding into another panic attack, making her muscles stiffen beneath his hands.

"Sweetheart, breathe," Teller whispered into her ear and stroked her hair at the same time, hoping that by holding her, he could help her work past the debilitating effects of her massive panic.

He held her in his arms, rocking back and forth as if he listened to music. Her fingers clenched and unclenched in the T-shirt. Slowly, her breathing became more regulated. Her sobs subsided, replaced by soft hiccups. Still, she clung to him, her body pressed to his.

Teller rested his chin on top of her head while rubbing her arms in an attempt to warm them from the instant chill she'd received while listening to the message.

When she finally calmed, but remained pressed into his chest, he squeezed her body gently and eased her away from him so that he could see her face and gauge her grasp on what was happening.

"I'm sorry," she said softly.

"Nothing to be sorry about," he assured her, his hand on her lower back, circling gently. All the questions he had could wait until she was able to answer them.

A few minutes later, she drew in a deep, slightly shaky breath and let it out slowly, deliberately. Then she stepped back.

Not until she was out of reach did Teller lower his arms. "Are you okay?"

"As okay as I can be, after seeing and hearing a ghost."

His brow pinched. "Huh?"

"At least, I thought I was seeing things. But now..." She tipped her head toward Teller's hand, which was holding her cell phone. "...I'm hearing things. The thing is, you heard it, too."

He didn't quite understand where she was going with her words. "I heard a male voice message from someone threatening you. What does that voicemail have to do with ghosts?"

"Exactly," she said with a soft snort. "Nothing. But you heard it, too. I didn't hallucinate the message like I thought I was hallucinating seeing a certain face on the streets of Honolulu, or outside the window of my office there. And now here."

"A certain face? You know this person?" Teller asked.

"That's the problem," she said, her eyes welling

with more tears. "The face I keep seeing is that of a former patient."

"And you think it's him stalking you?"

"Yes... No." She met his gaze. "You see, he committed suicide in my office. In front of me."

"Wow." Teller shook his head. "Not something you want to experience ever in your lifetime."

She nodded, her gaze on the floor in front of her. "One minute I'm talking with him. The next, he pulled out a gun, pressed it to his head and pulled the trigger."

He'd been with battle buddies who'd been mortally wounded. He'd held a good friend in his arms as his lifeblood and life flowed out of him. Watching a friend die had had a profound and lasting effect on him. He couldn't imagine the trauma of watching a patient shoot himself. "Are you sure he was dead?"

"I had brain matter and blood on me. When the emergency medical technicians arrived, they didn't even try to revive him. His face was basically gone." Sachie turned away, burying her face in her hands. "I can never unsee that image. Luke was only seventeen. He had his whole life ahead of him. Because I failed him, his life stopped."

"Sachie, did you pull the trigger?"

With her back still to him, she shook her head. "No. But I might as well have. I didn't do enough to help him understand that he was worthy, that his life mattered and that he could make anything of his future if he set his mind to it. He didn't see a way forward or an alternative to his pain and frustration. I could have—no, *should have*—been able to help him."

Teller tucked her cell phone in his pocket, gripped her shoulders and turned her toward him. "I've been in situations on the battlefield where, if I only made a different decision or been there a second earlier, one of my buddies wouldn't have died. Long afterward, I'd go over and over the scenario, wondering if I could've changed the outcome. Do you know what I learned?"

She shook her head.

"That no amount of second-guessing would bring them back."

"And the nightmares?" she asked.

He snorted softly. "I still have them. Just not as often."

"The nightmares are still so real," she said, her haunted gaze met his. "And when they happened during the day, I thought I was going crazy or hallucinating."

"How do you mean they happened during the day?" he asked.

"I'd be walking along the street, see a face so much like Luke's, and it would hit me so hard I couldn't breathe. When the face appeared in my window tonight, even though it was shadowed, it looked like him." She stared at Teller's chest. "I knew it couldn't be him because I was there when they carried him out of my office in a body bag. Then, the voice on the recording...sounded just like Luke." Her gaze returned to his. "How can that be?"

"Could it be someone's messing with you?" Teller brushed a strand of her hair off her cheek. "Did Luke have a friend or family member who looked like him?"

"He was an only child and didn't have many friends. He was moved around several times in the foster system after his father was incarcerated for murdering his mother."

"Tough break for a kid," Teller said. "No wonder he felt hopeless."

"He didn't want to be like his father and go off in blind rages."

"Now he's gone, do you think someone is blaming you for his death?"

"Based on the message," she said, "yes."

"Then either someone he knew cared that he died, or someone else is using his death as an excuse to terrorize you." He shook his head. "Either way, we need to find out who that is."

An alarm sounded from one of the cell phones in Teller's pockets. He dug out Sachie's and handed it to her. "It's yours."

She turned off the alarm, her lips twisting. "It's time to get up, get ready and go to work."

Teller frowned. "Can't you call in sick?"

Sachie shook her head. "In the short time I've been here, my schedule has quickly filled. Apparently, there aren't enough mental health professionals on the Big Island. I have to be there for them."

Teller didn't argue. If she had to go to work, he had to respect that. She cared about her patients.

"I have to change into more professional clothing," she said and headed for her bedroom again.

"Did you pack them in your suitcase?" Teller asked.

She stopped beside the suitcase she'd rolled into the hallway. "I packed some of my things. I think I have other clothes still hanging in the closet. I'll only be a few minutes."

Teller wandered down the hallway to the front door and examined the damage to the doorframe. He could fix it with the proper tools and supplies. Whoever had done this had been highly intent on getting inside and had been successful in breaking down both the front door and the door to Sachie's bedroom.

Had Teller been a few moments later, the attacker would have met Sachie and her butcher knife. He didn't even want to guess who would have won that fight.

"Kalea said she contacted someone to make the repairs on the house."

Teller turned around.

Sachie stood in the living room, dressed in a tailored medium-gray pantsuit and a soft rose-colored blouse. She'd pulled her hair up into a loose bun on top of her head with a few tendrils hanging down in front of each ear.

She'd gone from looking like a child in a T-shirt two times too large for her slim frame to a professional businesswoman. Where some women would look stuffy and boring in a pantsuit, Sachie looked so sexy. Teller had to shift his gaze to keep from ogling her.

"I know," she said. "Too much, isn't it? I don't normally dress so formally when working with kids and young adults, but I'm new at this practice, and I've been trying to make a good impression."

"You'll make a good impression," Teller said brusquely. "Are you ready?"

"I am," she said.

She gave him the address of the counseling center and followed him out to his vehicle.

Teller entered the address into the map program on his cell phone and connected it to the navigation screen in his SUV. As he pulled out onto the street, he looked both ways. "I'd like to stop by my apartment for a change of clothing," he said. "If you have time."

"I always try to arrive twenty to thirty minutes

early to review my case load to familiarize myself with the clients I will see that day," she said. "We're leaving early enough that we have the time to stop at your place."

"Perfectly commendable," Teller said. "I had a drill instructor who insisted that if you were on time, you were late."

"In what branch of service did you serve?" Sachie asked.

"Army," he replied.

"Special Operations?"

He nodded. "Delta Force."

"Thank you for your service," she said softly. "I understand Jace Hawkins hires former special operation types for the Brotherhood Protectors."

"That's right," Teller focused on the road ahead. "He has built an excellent team of former spec ops guys."

She glanced his way, her head tilted slightly, as she studied him. "Was it hard transitioning into civilian life?"

Teller shrugged. "Sometimes. It's so surreal that you're walking along a sidewalk and overhear someone complaining about having to work on a weekend or that the air conditioner in their car isn't working at its best capacity."

"We don't know how good we have it, do we?" Sachie said. "While we're worried about what to wear to the office, our men and women in uniform in a warzone are worried about missiles landing in the middle of their camp or being blown away by an improvised explosive device." She shook her head.

"Exactly." Teller's lips twisted. "I still duck when I hear loud noises."

"Or the sound of gunfire." Sachie sighed. "Which was a good thing when I ran out into the backyard like an idiot and you took me down."

He shot a crooked smile her way. "Sorry. I did what I had to do."

"Don't get me wrong," she said. "I'm glad you did. Thank you."

When they arrived at Teller's apartment, he glanced across the console at her. "I'll need you to come up to my apartment with me. I don't trust leaving you alone in the SUV."

Her brow furrowed as she glanced over her shoulder. "Were we followed?"

"Not that I could tell, but I don't want to risk it." He shifted into park and turned off the engine. "It won't take me long to grab a shirt."

"I'll come."

While Sachie unbuckled her seatbelt, Teller dropped down from the SUV and rounded the hood to the passenger side, scanning the cars, the hedges bordering the pavement and the road they'd just turned off. So far, so good.

Sachie had already pushed the door open when Teller arrived. He held out his hand.

When she laid her hand in Teller's palm, a jolt of electricity shot up his arm. Not used to having such a visceral reaction to touching a woman's hand, he quickly helped her to the ground and released his hold.

"I have to warn you, my place is a bachelor pad. It isn't the cleanest." He waved toward the walkway in front of him, indicating the way for her to go.

Once inside the apartment, he closed the door behind him and left Sachie standing in the entry. "I'll only be a minute."

He hurried into the single bedroom of the sparsely furnished unit and grabbed a T-shirt out of the chest of drawers.

"How long have you been in this apartment?" Sachie asked, her voice drifting through the open door.

"A couple of months." He pulled off the hula girl T-shirt, tossed it on the unmade bed and dragged on a clean dark shirt, much like the one he'd worn earlier. Before he left the room, he grabbed a gym bag and stuffed it with clean boxer briefs, a couple of shirts, jeans and socks. He used to have a go-bag ready at all times, stashed in his vehicle when he'd been in the military, never knowing when he'd be deployed. After last night, he figured it might be a good thing to start doing again, especially while working for the Brotherhood Protectors.

"Did you pick the furniture?" Sachie asked, the

sound coming from his living room instead of the front entry.

He stepped out of the bedroom, tugging the hem of his shirt down over his torso. "The apartment came furnished. It was only supposed to be temporary until I decided where I wanted to live."

She cocked an eyebrow. "And have you decided?"

He shook his head. "No. I've been all over this island and spent time on the Parkman Ranch, which is amazing, but I haven't really looked for a more permanent place to live. I was thinking of visiting the other islands before I made up my mind."

Sachie crossed to the window overlooking another apartment complex that had seen better days. "What are you looking for in a permanent home?"

He snorted. "I don't know. I've never had a permanent home."

She turned back, a frown denting her forehead. "What about when you were growing up?"

Teller usually didn't talk about his distant past. There wasn't much to talk about. "I didn't have a permanent home." He waved a hand toward the door. "We'd better get you to your office."

Sachie opened her mouth as if to say something and then closed it. "Right. I need to get to work." She walked past him to the door. She didn't say anything as he carried the gym bag out to his SUV and tossed it in next to her suitcase. The silence continued as he drove through the streets of Hilo.

He'd consigned memories of his life before he'd joined the Army to the back of his mind. Having been part of the foster care system since he was eleven, he hadn't had a place he could call home. Before foster care, his father had been enlisted in the Army. They'd moved four times before his eleventh birthday. When his father, mother and sister had died in an automobile crash, he'd lost any chance of a permanent home. He would have died in that crash as well if he had been wearing his seat belt. Many times throughout the rest of his childhood, he'd wished he had died.

The guilt he lived with made him act out with each of the many foster homes he'd been shuffled around to.

A siren sounded behind him, yanking him out of his past and into the present. Just ahead of them, a fire engine pulled out of a station house onto the road.

Teller slowed to let the huge truck make the turn, heading in the same direction as they were.

The engine picked up speed, the siren wailing now, lights flashing.

Teller gave the truck a decent amount of space before he continued along the road. A glance at the map indicated they were nearing Sachie's office.

Over the top of the fire engine, a plume of sooty gray smoke rose into the air.

"Oh my God," Sachie leaned forward in her seat. "That's my office! It's on fire!"

Teller pulled into the parking lot of an auto parts store a couple of blocks short of Sachie's office.

"Why are you stopping here?" she demanded. "My office is up there. On fire."

"And we need to stay clear and let the fire department do what they're trained to do," Teller said. "There might be more trucks and emergency vehicles on the way."

As if to prove Teller's point, a police car roared by on the street and stopped a block short of the fire. The officer then turned his vehicle sideways in the street, blocking the oncoming traffic.

The fire engine was parked in the middle of the street. Men in fire-resistant suits jumped down and unrolled hoses from the truck, hurrying to attach one end to a fire hydrant.

"I'm going to get closer," Sachie pushed open her door and jumped down from the SUV.

Teller quickly followed suit, racing to catch up to her before she reached the burning building.

Before they could get close, the police officer blocking the street held up his hands. "You'll need to stay back until they get that fire under control."

"That's my office," Sachie cried.

The roof of the building chose that moment to crash in, sending a cloud of smoke and glowing cinders into the air.

The officer glanced over his shoulder and shook his head. "Not anymore."

Sachie stood in the middle of the street, her shoulders drooping and her eyes welling with tears. "What's happening?"

Teller slipped his arm around her waist and pulled her against him. Teller didn't have an answer for her, but he sure as hell would find out.

# CHAPTER 5

AFTER SACHIE HAD SPENT hours watching the fire department put out the fire and talking to the fire chief and the police, suddenly they were done. She wasn't needed. She couldn't sift through the rubble until they'd conducted a thorough investigation to identify the source of the blaze. The fire chief and the police told her she could go.

But to where?

Going back to her cottage was out of the question. The office where she'd set up her practice was gone. She'd ended her lease on her apartment in Honolulu. She had nowhere to go.

As if she could read her friend's mind, Kalea called. "Teller told us what happened."

Tears filled Sachie's eyes. "I was just trying to decide where to go from here."

"You're coming to Parkman Ranch. Teller will drive you here. You can stay as long as you need to."

"I can't do that," Sachie said. "I've already brought trouble to the island. I won't bring it to your doorstep. You're eight months pregnant. You don't need that kind of stress."

"I'd be more stressed not knowing whether or not you're safe," Kalea said. "Besides, security on the ranch has never been better. I insist you come and stay."

"Just say yes," Teller whispered into her ear.

"You knew about this?" Sachie looked up into his eyes, suddenly realizing just how close he was. Her heart fluttered and then raced, making her forget what she was about to say.

"I've been texting with Hawk," Teller said. "He wants you to come as well. At least for a couple of nights until we come up with a plan."

Her frown deepened. "I'd never forgive myself if anything happened to Kalea and her baby."

"Nothing's going to happen," Kalea said into her ear, bringing Sachie back to the conversation. "The regional office of the Brotherhood Protectors is located here. They have access to computers, databases and anything you might need to figure out who is making your life a living hell. It's decided. Teller will get you here in time for lunch. I'll see you then. And you can help me pick out what color to paint the nursery. I can fly a plane and help run this ranch, but I'm hopeless at interior decorating. See you soon."

Before Sachie could say anything to the contrary, the call ended. She looked up into Teller's serious face. "I guess we're going to Parkman Ranch."

A smile tipped the corners of his lips. "Good. We have more resources there to start this investigation."

"That's what Kalea said." Her eyes narrowed. "And I want to find the bastard who's doing this to me and put an end to this nonsense."

"Then let's go. The sooner we get there, the sooner we can start working on a plan." He cupped her elbow and led her to his SUV, where they'd left it in front of the auto parts store.

Even before they got there, they could see that the SUV wasn't how they'd left it. Deeply scratched into the side of the door were jagged words.

*YOU FAILED ME!*

Sachie clapped a hand over her mouth and stopped. "Oh, Teller. I'm so sorry."

His lips had thinned into a tight line, and his jaw had hardened to the point it twitched. "You have nothing to be sorry about. Someone else did this. Not you." He glanced around at the store and pointed. "They've got a security camera. Let's check it out."

Sachie marched with him into the parts store, praying the camera would give them a clear image of the person stalking her.

A bell rang over the door as they entered.

The young man behind the counter couldn't have been more than nineteen. He looked up from his cell phone. "Good morning. Can I help you, or are you just interested in information about the fire down the road?"

"Have many people been in here since the fire started?" Sachie asked, leaning forward to read the man's name tag, and added, "Johnny."

The guy shrugged. "There have been more vehicles in the parking lot than usual, but mostly to turn around and head back the other direction. Is there something I can get you?"

"I was one of the people who parked in your parking lot," Teller said. "Someone keyed my door while we were checking out the fire."

Johnny held up his hands. "I don't think we're liable for damage to vehicles parked in our parking lot. You'd have to take it up with the manager. I just work here."

"Is your manager in?" Teller asked.

Johnny shook his head. "He got a call saying they had a shipment to pick up at the airport. He left half an hour ago."

"We're not interested in suing the store for the damage. But we are interested in finding out who did it." Teller tipped his head toward the entrance. "I noticed there's a camera on the front of the store. Do you have a security system installed?"

"Yeah, it's new, but it's really awesome," he said

excitedly and turned to the computer monitor on the counter. "We can pull up the videos from any of the computers."

Sachie leaned her elbows on the counter. "Can you pull up recordings from that front camera for the past two or three hours?"

"Sure can." Johnny ran his fingers across the keypad, his brow furrowing in concentration. "It might take me a minute or two. My manager only showed me yesterday, and I haven't had a chance to play with it since." He turned the monitor halfway around so that Teller and Sachie could see the screen while he pulled up a menu and selected an application.

An array of live images popped up on the screen.

"It's displaying real-time now," Johnny said, pointing to the image on the left of the screen. "That's the camera mounted on the front of the building."

"You can see my SUV," Teller said. "The black one on the corner of the lot, closest to the street."

Johnny enlarged the image from the front camera to fill the entire screen. He squinted at the monitor. "I don't see anything scratched into the side panel. Is it on the other side?"

"Yes," Teller said. "On the passenger side."

"Can you rewind it to display the past few hours?" Sachie asked. "Maybe we can see who was hanging around long enough to scratch words into the paint."

"I can try," Johnny said, frowning in concentration as he used the mouse to move the cursor over several tabs, not finding what he was looking for. Finally, he hovered the cursor over the outside image itself, and a sliding bar appeared. "How far back do you want to take it?"

"Start when we got here, about three hours ago," Teller said.

Johnny slid the bar to the left, backing the time up to three hours before, and then hit the play button. The video moved forward at normal speed.

"Can you fast-forward?" Sachie asked. "At a pace we can still see what's happening?"

"I can try," Johnny fiddled with the different options, finally finding one that would play the video at whatever speed they chose. After several tries, they got the speed up where they could see vehicles coming and going and people getting out of parked cars and trucks to either enter the store or walk down the street toward the fire. An hour of the video sped by in three minutes, and nothing jumped out at them. No one moved toward the SUV during that time. Several vehicles pulled out of the parking lot on that end, but none slowed long enough for someone to jump out, scratch words into the paint and get back in without capturing their attention.

"Please, keep going," Teller urged the kid.

The bell over the door jingled, drawing Johnny's attention. "I have to help customers."

"Do you mind if we keep watching?" Sachie asked.

The young man shrugged. "I don't. My manager might." He slipped the mouse across the counter toward Sachie. "I'll be right back." He left to help a customer find a replacement key fob for his truck.

Sachie took control of the mouse and started the video moving forward again at a swift clip. Another thirty minutes passed, and still nothing.

Johnny rang up the customer's purchase, thanked him and waited until he'd left the store before returning to Sachie and Teller. "Anything?"

"Not yet," Sachie said.

At that point, a delivery truck pulled in front of the store and stopped, blocking the camera's view of the rest of the parking lot.

Several minutes passed as the driver got out, opened the rear doors of the truck and climbed into the back. He stacked several boxes onto a dolly, rolled the dolly to a hydraulic lift and lowered it to the ground. Then he wheeled the boxes into the store.

"Is it normal to receive shipments through the front of the store at that time of day?" Teller asked.

Johnny's brow twisted. "The time's about right, but they usually deliver through the rear door. I remember telling the guy he should've taken the boxes through the back door. He said someone had blocked the back alley. He couldn't take his truck through."

"Can you bring up the back alley camera for that time?" Sachie asked.

"Sure," Johnny said and took control of the mouse. Moments later, they had a view of the rear of the store. Nothing seemed to be blocking the back of the store. "But that alley serves more than just this store. Someone could've parked at the end."

"Do any of the other stores that use that alley have security systems?" Teller asked.

Johnny snorted. "I doubt it. One is a laundry service. The other sells fancy bird feeders and seed."

"Let's go back to the front camera," Sachie said.

Johnny filled the monitor with the front camera's video, and they played it all the way to the current time, finding nothing more of interest.

Teller shook his head. "Whoever did it must have known there was a camera on the store and did his damage while the delivery truck was here." He held out his hand to Johnny. "Thank you for letting us look through the video. We had to try."

"I'm sorry you weren't able to find the guy, and I'm sorry your vehicle was damaged." Johnny shook Teller's hand and let go. "Do you want me to bring it to the manager's attention?" Maybe the store has liability insurance that would cover it."

"That won't be necessary," Teller said. "My insurance will cover it."

"I'll look through more of the footage," Johnny

offered. "If I see anything that sticks out, I could let you know."

Teller dug a card out of his wallet and handed it to the young clerk. "Thanks, Johnny. You've been a big help."

"Wish I could have done more," he said, staring down at the information on Teller's card. "Hey, I've heard about the Brotherhood Protectors. They're a group of prior military guys, aren't they?"

Teller nodded. "Yes, we are."

Johnny glanced up, a grin spreading across his face. "I talked with an Army recruiter last week. I'm enlisting at the end of this month. Do you have any words of wisdom you'd care to share?

Teller met the young man's gaze. "No matter what you do in life, do your very best. Your buddies you fight alongside are your brothers. Have their backs, and they'll have yours."

"I will." Johnny stood straighter. "Thank you, sir."

Sachie could feel the pride Teller had for his time in the service and the pride Johnny had for his chosen commitment.

They left the store and headed for the SUV.

Sachie grimaced at the scratched words on the side of the vehicle and started to say she was sorry again.

Teller held the door for her and gave her a stern look. "It's not your fault."

"It wouldn't have happened if you hadn't taken me on. The least I can do is pay to have it fixed."

"Like I told Johnny," he said as he helped her up into her seat. "Insurance will cover it."

Sachie buckled her seat belt as Teller rounded the front of the SUV and slid into the driver's seat.

"Whoever attacked me at my house and set fire to my office had to have known we parked here at the parts store," Sachie said.

Teller paused with his hand on the gear shift. "He could've followed us from your house."

"He had to have started the fire earlier, then hurried back to my house, followed us to your apartment and then to the store." Wouldn't the office have burned all the way to the ground by then?" Sachie stared across the cab at Teller, trying to make sense of the timeline. "The fire truck was just getting to the fire when we were almost there."

Sachie frowned. "Could he have tagged your SUV with a tracking device?"

"Maybe." Teller left the SUV in park and climbed out.

Sachie got out of her side and ducked low, searching for anything attached to the vehicle that didn't look like it belonged.

Teller slid beneath the chassis and inspected the underbelly.

When he stood, he shook his head. "If he tagged it,

he could have removed he device when he scratched the words into the door."

"Thanks for looking," Sachie said. "I'd rather not lead him out to Parkman Ranch, even if Kalea assured me they have a great security system."

They got back into the SUV and buckled their seatbelts.

Teller backed out of the parking space and pulled out onto the street, heading for the highway that would lead them to the ranch.

"Teller," Sachie said after they left Hilo behind. "I don't want to stay too long at the ranch. I don't want anything to happen to Kalea and her baby."

He nodded. "Understood. We'll come up with a plan tonight and leave first thing in the morning."

She drew in a deep breath and let it out slowly. "Thank you."

He shot her a tight smile. "We'll figure this out."

"I hope we do, before anyone gets hurt any worse than a flesh wound."

Several miles passed in silence.

"Tell me about what happened that made you move to the Big Island," Teller said. "Were you experiencing incidents similar to what has happened since you got here?"

Sachie thought through everything that had happened since Luke's suicide.

"It started as a feeling of being watched all the

time. I'd be walking through normal places like a grocery store or shopping mall and feel like someone was watching me. When I turned around, no one was there. My phone would ring, but when I answered, no one was on the other end. Once, I walked by a building with big windows and thought I saw the reflection of someone following me. Again, when I turned around, no one was there. At first, I counted it off as residual trauma from what happened in my office."

"What pushed you so far that you felt you had to move?"

She closed her eyes, and she was back at her apartment building, inserting her key in the lock. It worked like it always had, and she pushed through the door. "I walked into my apartment one day, and something wasn't right. A coffee cup stood in the middle of the living room floor. The photograph of my family and me wasn't on the end table by the sofa. I found it in the oven. When I went into the bedroom, my pillows were gone from my bed. They were in the bathtub, and it was filled with water."

Sachie shivered at the memory.

"Any messages?"

"No," she said.

"So, if it's the same guy, he followed you here, and it's escalating."

"Yeah." Sachie stared out the windshield at the road ahead. "I'm tired of being the victim."

"Then let's turn it around." Teller extended his hand across the console.

She laid her palm in his. "I'm ready."

# CHAPTER 6

AT THE GATE to the Parkman Ranch, a camera in the arched gate pointed down at them where they waited in the SUV.

Teller pressed a button to notify the ranch's security personnel of their arrival.

Sachie had visited the ranch before to see Kalea. She knew it had a first-class security system. Still, she didn't want to be there any longer than was necessary to come up with a plan to out her stalker.

The gate opened, and Teller drove the winding road over a small hill and through a stand of trees, finally climbing a rise to a sprawling ranch house.

As soon as they pulled to a stop, Kalea and Hawk came out on the porch. Kalea wore a maternity dress covered in a bright pink and green hibiscus pattern. She'd secured her long, wavy hair in a loose bun at the crown of her head.

Her heart full of love for her friend, Sachie climbed down from the SUV and hurried up the steps to hug her. "You look amazing."

Kalea laughed. "Amazingly big?"

"Not at all," Sachie said and then smiled. "Well, maybe a little. You are, after all, eight months pregnant. What I meant was you absolutely glow. How are you feeling?"

"Good," Kalea said. "But I should be asking you that. What the hell is going on?"

Teller climbed the steps of the porch, carrying her suitcase and his gym bag.

Hawk reached for the suitcase with one hand and held out the other to shake Teller's. "Thanks for responding to my call in the middle of the night."

"I'm glad I did." Teller nodded toward Sachie. "We don't want to be here more than a night, but we could use some help coming up with a plan. I was hoping we could put our heads together with you, Hank Patterson and his computer guy, Swede."

Hawk nodded and held open the front door. "Let's take it inside and get you two settled. I gave Patterson and Swede a heads-up that we'd be calling them after lunch. They're on standby to help us in way they can."

"I had our chef prepare soup and sandwiches," Kalea said. "We can eat in the dining room or take it all to the war room."

"Though we haven't had breakfast or lunch, I'd

like to get Hank and Swede briefed as soon as possible," Teller said.

Sachie nodded. "Me, too."

"Then we'll serve lunch in the war room," Kalea said.

"Let me take your bags up to your rooms." Hawk took the gym bag from Teller. "I'll show you where they are when you're ready to go up. You both know the way to the offices and the war room. I'll join you in a minute."

Kalea moved ahead of them. "I'll let Ule know to move the meal to the Brotherhood Protectors outbuilding."

"If it's going to be that much trouble, we can wait to eat when we're done in the war room," Sachie insisted.

"Ule won't mind." Kalea smiled. "And I'll make sure he has help."

Sachie's eyes widened. "As long as that help isn't you."

Kalea's smile twisted. "I've been strictly forbidden to lift and carry anything heavier than a cup of tea and banned from riding and flying until after the baby is born." She patted her belly. "I'm bored out of my mind."

Sachie laughed. "Not for much longer."

Kalea sighed. "I know, and I can't wait for him or her to arrive."

"You still don't know what you're having?" Sachie asked.

"Hawk and I decided to wait." Kalea frowned. "Which makes choosing a paint color for the nursery impossible. But more on that after your meeting and lunch. Go. I'll be out there soon."

Teller and Sachie passed through the house and out the back door.

One of the outbuildings had been remodeled and equipped with state-of-the-art computers, satellite systems, offices, a war room and an armory.

"You've been here before?" Teller asked.

Sachie nodded. "Once."

"Have you met Hank Patterson or Axel Svenson, aka Swede?"

"No, but Kalea talks about them all the time. She and Hawk have a lot of confidence in them and the rest of the Brotherhood Protectors around the world."

When they arrived at the building, Teller pressed his thumb to a biometric reader. A moment later, a lock clicked. Teller opened the door and stood back to let Sachie enter first.

She led the way into the war room, where a long conference table took up the center of the room with a huge screen at one end.

Teller crossed to the array of monitors on one side of the room and touched a mouse. The monitors blinked awake from their sleep mode and brought up images from security cameras.

"Can you tell if anyone followed us?" Sachie asked.

Teller shook his head. "No, but they have a security team monitoring the access road at all times. They would alert Hawk, Kalea and Mr. Parkman if there was a breach or suspicious behavior around the property."

Footsteps sounded from the hallway.

Sachie turned in time to find Ule, Mr. Parkman's chef, carrying a large tray filled with sandwiches, utensils, bowls and crackers. Behind him came Hawk carrying a soup tureen, which he carefully set on the conference table.

Kalea brought up the rear with a roll of paper towels. "See?" She held up the roll with a grimace. "They wouldn't let me carry anything heavier than a cup of tea or a roll of paper towels. Way to make a girl feel useless."

"We're headed into the last couple of weeks of your pregnancy." Hawk slipped an arm around his wife's waist. "We only want what's best for the health of you and the baby." He dropped a kiss on the top of her head.

Kalea snorted. "What about my mental health? I'm a doer. I need to be doing."

"When that baby comes, we'll all be doing," Hawk reminded her. "You can help Ule lay out the food for everyone while I bring Hank and Swede online." He stepped away from Kalea and joined Teller at the computer.

Sachie helped Ule and Kalea arrange plates on the table, ladle soup into bowls and uncover the selection of different types of sandwiches. Her stomach rumbled, reminding her she hadn't eaten since the night before.

Her gaze went to Teller.

He turned in time to capture her glance with his.

A surge of awareness rippled through Sachie. The man really was good-looking in a quiet, brooding way. She wanted to know more about him and his statement that he'd never had a permanent home. What was his background? She knew so little about him. That didn't seem to matter. She trusted him to keep her safe. Hell, he'd saved her life once already.

The large screen at the end of the monitor flickered to life with the matching desktop image of what was on the computer monitor in front of Hawk and Teller. The display flickered, and the faces of two men appeared who seemed to be talking, though no sound accompanied the movement of their lips.

A moment later, their voices came through loud and clear.

"Can you hear me now?" the dark-haired man asked.

Sachie nodded.

Teller and Hawk joined Sachie and Kalea at the table.

Hawk pulled out a chair for Kalea. She sank gratefully into the seat and reached for one of the sandwiches. "You'll have to forgive us for eating in front of you," she said to the men, joining them virtually. "If you were here, I'd offer you a plate."

"Thank you, Kalea," the dark-haired one said. "Not much longer, is it?"

"Three to four weeks," she said. "How are Sadie and the little ones?"

"Sadie's doing great. She's on hiatus until the end of the year," the man said. "Emma's going to preschool this fall, and McClain is walking."

"That's great." Kalea smiled and turned toward Sachie. "Sachie, the dark-haired man on the left is Hank Patterson. The one on the right is everyone's favorite computer guru, Axel Svenson aka Swede."

Sachie dipped her head. "Nice to finally meet you both. I've heard so many good things about you and the Brotherhood Protectors since Hawk arrived in the islands."

"Glad to hear it," Patterson said. "We try to provide the help people need."

Sachie gave the man a weak smile. "Like me?"

Hank nodded. "Yes, ma'am. How's Osgood working out for you?"

Sachie glanced across the conference table to

Teller. "Good," she said. "He saved my life in his first five minutes on duty."

"I'm glad he was able to get to you in time," Hank said. "Perhaps you could fill us in on what's happened thus far. Start with why you moved from Oahu to the Big Island. Hawk tells us you had issues there."

Sachie gave Hank a brief description of what she'd experienced on Oahu and her move to the Big Island to escape the threats and start over. "I thought I was past it when I woke up from a bad dream, saw a face in the window, discovered my car windshield smashed and someone trying to break into my cottage."

Teller picked up from there, relating how he'd come into the house, chased the assailant out the back door and then came back to look for Sachie.

"That's when I made first contact with your Brotherhood Protector," Sachie's lips twisted, "and tried to kill him."

Hank chuckled. "I'm glad you didn't succeed."

"As am I," Sachie said. "He took a bullet for me a minute later." She nodded toward Teller.

"Just a flesh wound," Teller said and continued with the message on Sachie's cell phone, their arrival on the street where Sachie's office was burning to the ground, their conversations with the police and fire chief, the message scratched into the side of his SUV and their search on the security camera footage. "And that's how we came to be at the Parkman Ranch," he finished.

Hank's brow furrowed. "Tell me again what the messages said."

"You failed me," Sachie said. "On the cell phone and on the car."

"With the added note of *Now you will pay* on the voicemail message," Teller said.

"You're a counselor who works with troubled teens?"

Sachie nodded. "I've worked with teens to help them with PTSD from abusive environments or who have addiction issues. I've worked with the police to remove children from unsafe home environments."

"Could your stalker be one of your patients?" Hank asked.

I wasn't sure when I was in Honolulu, because there was never a message, just actions. I was working through some issues of my own."

"Hawk told us," Hank said softly. "I'm sorry that happened to you."

"I'm sorry it happened to my patient," Sachie said, her eyes filling with tears. "The messages I've received only reinforce how I feel about that situation." She drew in a breath and let it out. "I failed him."

"Your patient died that day," Hank stated. "Did he have any relatives who might blame you?"

Sachie shook her head. "He entered the foster care

system when his father murdered his mother in a fit of rage. For seven years, he was passed around from home to home and ended up getting in with the wrong crowd at school and caught with illegal drugs. That's when I started seeing him. Based on everything he told us, the psychiatrist I worked with diagnosed him as bipolar. He was on medication to help him control it. He seemed to be doing better for a while; he had a girlfriend, was working after school at the Boys' Club and his grades had improved. Then he became more sullen at our weekly meetings. I thought he might be back into drugs. When he came in that last day, he was distraught, claiming he'd put his girlfriend in the hospital. He didn't want to be like his father. Didn't want to kill the person he was supposed to love."

"Did she die?" Hank asked. "The girlfriend?"

Sachie shook her head. "No. She recovered from a concussion."

"Did you talk with her?" Swede asked.

"No," Sachie said. "Her parents were keeping her on suicide watch and didn't want anyone to remind her Luke had killed himself."

"Are there any other patients or parents of patients who might feel you failed them?" Swede asked.

Sachie's eyes narrowed. "I worked with the Honolulu PD on cases where children needed to be removed from abusive homes. The parents were never happy about it."

"Do any of them stand out more in your mind than others?" Teller asked.

"I was in court the week before Luke..." She stopped, drew in a breath and continued. "I had to testify against a woman who let her boyfriend use her little girl as a punching bag. She yelled obscenities in the courtroom."

"Did she threaten you specifically?" Swede asked.

Sachie nodded. "She blamed me for her boyfriend being taken to jail and her daughter being removed from her custody. She said I'd regret the day I ruined her life."

"Do you have the name of that woman?" Swede persisted.

Sachie shook her head. "My memory since Luke's death hasn't been the best. I need to access the files back at my old office in Honolulu." She pushed a hand through her hair. "I'm sorry, I'm not much help."

"Is it possible to access the data from your patient files online?" Swede asked.

"Maybe...?" she answered. "I'd have to get permission from the owner of the practice, since I'm not an employee anymore."

"We could start there," Teller said softly. "Maybe going through the files will trigger a memory of another patient who might have shown violent tendencies recently."

"I'll call the office and see what I can do to get access," Sachie said. "Although I really feel like I'd be closer to answers if I returned to Honolulu."

Kalea laid a hand on Sachie's arm. "Oh, Sachie, you can't go back there. We need you on the Big Island."

"Not if I don't have an office." Sachie patted Kalea's hand on her arm. "I can't stay here. No matter how robust your security system might be, I couldn't live with myself if whoever is after me hurts you while trying to get to me."

"At least stay a few days," Kalea begged. "I could use some female companionship while I wait out the last month of this pregnancy."

"As much as I'd love to spend time with you, I can't risk it," Sachie said. "I've told you all I know for now. I'll make the call to my former boss and ask for access to the online files. We can take it from there. Though I must warn you that patient records are confidential. I couldn't share much."

"We'll work with you on that." Hank gave her a gentle smile. "I know it's a lot to take in after all you've been through, but we need to know enough about the people you came into contact with who might blame you for whatever happened to them or their kid."

Teller cleared his throat. "Someone might want

revenge against the well-meaning counselor who put her boyfriend in jail, or a patient you might've blown the whistle on for getting back into drugs."

"If you get that permission to access your patient files online or think of anything else that might give us a starting point, let us know immediately," Swede said. "I'll answer day or night."

Sachie gave the computer guru a tired smile. "I will—and thank you for helping me."

"That's what we do," Hank said softly. "In the meantime, Osgood will be with you until the situation is resolved. Hawk...Osgood, do you have anything to add?"

The two men shook their heads.

"Then we're out here," Hank said.

"Out here," Hawk echoed.

Hank and Swede's faces disappeared, replaced by a blue screen.

Sachie placed the call to her former boss and got his voicemail. She left a message asking him to call her back as soon as he received her message. When she finished her message, she slipped her cell phone into her pocket and looked around at the expectant faces.

"Now we wait for his response. In the meantime, I can't just sit around and wait for my phone to ring," she said and turned to Kalea. "Show me the nursery and the color swatches."

Sachie followed Kalea back to the house, her

mind on all the patients or family members of patients she'd worked with recently who might want her dead.

# CHAPTER 7

Teller and Hawk exited the outbuilding and watched as Kalea and Sachie walked slowly up to the house. Once the women were inside, the men wandered over to a fence and looked out over the pasture beyond.

"Thanks for answering the call last night," Hawk said. "Kalea wanted me to jump in my truck and race into Hilo to help her friend."

Teller shook his head, his gaze on the pasture and the horses grazing peacefully in it. "You would've been too late. The intruder was working on breaking down her bedroom door when I arrived, and he was armed."

Hawk leaned his arms on the top rail of the fence. "There have been many times throughout my career as a Navy SEAL, and now as a Brotherhood Protector, when I felt I was in the right place at the right time." He tipped his head toward the house. "When I was given Kalea as my first assignment as a protector, I wasn't keen on the role of an undercover bodyguard to a spoiled little rich girl." He grinned. "She gave me a run for my money. I thought my timing was off on that one, but in the end, it was spot on. I was meant to be there for her." He grinned. "And I couldn't be happier."

Teller's thoughts went to the woman he'd been sent to protect. His pulse raced as he recalled the broken doorframes and how close she'd come to coming face-to-face with a man who might have killed her. He was glad he'd gotten there before that could happen. And now that he'd spent a little time with Sachie, he found he wanted to spend more. Working with troubled teens and children in horribly abusive situations had to be hard. It took a strong individual to deal with all she had to do. He respected her for taking on that kind of work. "I'm glad I was there," he said and then chuckled. "Although Ms. Moore might've come out of that attack all right. She's wicked with a butcher knife."

"Kalea says Sachie grew up in an abusive home," Hawk said.

Teller's breath hung in his lungs. "Really?"

Hawk nodded. "She went into her career field fully intending to help kids like herself realize they could have a better life. When the young man took his life, it hit Sachie hard. Kalea would have gone to her immediately, but her father and I wouldn't let her."

Wow. He had more in common with the feisty counselor than he could have imagined. "There aren't enough counselors willing to take on troubled teens," he said, knowing the truth of it. He'd never had a counselor to help him through his teen years when he'd been so angry at the world, his hormones exacerbating his moods. He'd overheard his foster parents talking about him. Joe, the man of the house, had argued with his wife. He'd told his wife that Teller would never amount to anything if he didn't get his shit together. Most likely, he'd end up joining a gang and dying in a gutter from an overdose.

Joe had had little patience for Teller's moody aggression and had smacked him around whenever he'd reached his limit.

Teller had taken all he could. He'd packed a few items into his school backpack and was on his way out of their lives when he'd overheard that conversation. He'd started to storm out of the house and never look back. As he'd reached for the doorknob, he'd realized he'd end up exactly as Joe predicted. With no job, no place to live and no money, he would be on a downhill track.

He crept back up the stairs to his room, unpacked his backpack and settled in to do the homework he'd tossed in the trash. From that moment on, he'd kept out of trouble, not for Joe, but for himself, and finished high school. As soon as he'd had his diploma in hand, he'd joined the Army and left his past behind him, determined to prove Joe wrong. What he'd accomplished was proving to himself he could do anything he set his mind to.

"You've been there, haven't you?" Hawk said quietly.

Teller shot a glance toward Hawk. How did he know?

Of course. Swede was an expert hacker and could tap into any database. Hank had probably performed a thorough background check on each person he invited to become a Brotherhood Protector. Teller couldn't blame him. His reputation depended on the reliability of his agents. Not only his reputation, but also the lives of his clients.

Teller nodded. "As you know, my childhood wasn't the greatest."

"Yet you overcame it, and you're stronger for having worked so hard to make it better. Not only were you at the right place at the right time, but you were also the right person to help Sachie. Of all the members of our team, you understand her and her mission better than anyone." Hawk clapped him on the back. "Shall we join the ladies and see what color they've chosen for the nursery, which I'll likely have to paint tomorrow?"

Teller entered the ranch house behind Hawk with an even deeper appreciation for his client. He could only imagine the kind of abuse Sachie had endured in her childhood. He hoped that someday she would trust him enough to know he would never hurt her in any way.

They found Sachie, Kalea and Mr. Parkman in the big farm kitchen, seated at a table large enough for a dozen people. Each had a glass of lemonade in their hands, sipping and talking about colors, fabrics and what Kalea had packed in her go-bag for when she went into labor. At least the women were talking. Mr. Parkman sat in uncomfortable silence, pretending to be interested.

As soon as Hawk and Teller entered the room, Mr. Parkman looked up in relief. "Thought you'd never show up. The womenfolk have discussed the nursery room design until I'm blue in the face. Anyone want to see if there's a ballgame on? Or maybe some wrestling?"

"Actually, I'd love to watch some wrestling," Kalea said. "All this talk about babies and nurseries has worn me out." She lurched to her feet. "I'll meet you in the living room after I make a detour to the bathroom. The baby is pressing heavily on my bladder."

"Popcorn or pretzels?" her father asked, heading for the pantry.

"Popcorn," Kelea answered promptly. "Pretzels go with beer. I won't be drinking beer until this kid is weaned." Kalea sighed. "The sacrifices we women have to make."

Hawk dropped a kiss on the top of her hair. "You're going to be an amazing mother."

"And you're going to change diapers and feed the baby in the middle of the night when I'm so exhausted I can't remember what's up and what's down."

"Yes, ma'am. I've been practicing diaper changing on the baby's stuffed bear. I've got it down to five seconds flat."

"Yeah, yeah," Kelea said as she left the room. "Wait until you change a moving target."

Hawk chuckled. "I can't wait." He took the popcorn packet from Mr. Parkman, tore off the cellophane and placed the bag in the microwave. "Are you two going to watch the match with us?"

Sachie glanced toward the window. "If you don't mind, I'd like to go out and enjoy what's left of the afternoon sunshine."

"I'll go with you," Teller said.

Sachie walked out the back door, stood for a moment on the deck and drew in a deep breath. She let it out slowly and turned to Teller. "Care to take a walk?"

"Sure," he responded.

"You know, it's safe here on the ranch. Don't feel obligated to follow me around. If you'd rather watch the match with Kalea and her family, you won't hurt my feelings."

He touched a hand to her back and descended the

steps to the ground. "I'd love to go for a walk. The sun is still shining, and the air is fresh."

"That's how I feel. It would be nice to clear the smell of smoke from my system." She headed toward the fence where he'd stood minutes before with Hawk, discussing her. She climbed up on the first rail and placed her foot on the second.

"Were your ears burning?" Teller asked.

"What?" Sachie lost her grip on the top rail and fell backward.

Teller easily caught her, one arm behind her back and the other beneath her knees.

She glared at him without fighting to free herself of his hold. "Were you and Hawk talking about me?"

"You were part of the conversation." Teller's lips twitched, and his brow twisted. "And he talked a lot about timing and how it worked for him and Kalea, though he hadn't really wanted to be her protector in the very beginning." He shook his head. "I'm not certain what point he was trying to make." He hefted her up onto the top rail and gripped her knees until she had her balance. "Got it?"

She nodded. "Yeah. You can let go."

He did but remained at the ready in case she tipped one way or the other.

"What were you and Hawk saying about me?"

"He told me you had a difficult childhood, and that working as a counselor was your way of helping others with similar challenges." Teller didn't go into detail about what difficulties she'd encountered growing up. If she wanted him to know, she would tell him. If not, it was none of his business.

She turned, swung a leg over the top rail, straddling the fence, her gaze going out to pasture where the horse still grazed, unconcerned about humans and their hangups. "You were part of the conversation in the nursery as well," Sachie said.

"Were you so stuck for interesting conversation that you had to resort to talking about me?" he asked, surprised his name had come up. If he were honest with himself, he was a bit flattered and curious.

She nodded. "Kalea said you were one of the team members who'd been hardest to get to know. She thought maybe you'd been hurt by someone in the past. A wife, girlfriend, family member, and that it gave you trust issues." Sachie looked back at Teller.

Teller leaned his elbows on the fence in front of her knees and stared out at the field. "What do you think?"

"That it's none of my business," she said.

"Have you ever lost trust in someone?"

"Who hasn't?" She looked away.

"I didn't lose trust in a wife," he said. "I've never been married."

Sachie glanced down at him, her brow furrowing. "Never? A good-looking guy like you?"

He liked that she found him attractive, but didn't say anything, not wanting to lead her on.

"Did a girlfriend let you down?" Sachie asked. "Sorry. Just curious. You don't have to answer that."

"I dated, but never for long. You see, I lost trust in family as a unit. My parents and my little sister died in a car crash. I was the only one to survive the wreck, and only because I'd unbuckled my seatbelt and rolled down my window. My parents were arguing over whether or not I should roll up the window when a semi tractor-trailer rig crossed the median and ran into us. If I hadn't rolled down that window, my parents wouldn't have been arguing. My dad might've seen the semi coming at us and swerved in time to miss it. As it was, I was thrown clear. The car flipped several times, crushing my father, mother and sister inside. With no living relatives to take me in, I was dumped into foster care. I stayed with seven families in the eight years I was part of that system. I suffered from survivor's guilt and acted out. I should've died in that wreck."

Sachie touched his arm. "What did you tell me? You didn't pull the trigger. You weren't driving that truck. It wasn't your fault."

"Maybe it was." Teller shrugged. "I didn't believe in family for so long that when I joined the Army, I'd been a loner for so long, it was hard to integrate as part of a team. Once I did, I found the family I'd longed for in my brothers in arms. I didn't need anyone else."

"And now?"

"My team is scattered over the islands, but I know they're there. They'll always have my back."

"What about love?"

Teller nodded. "I love my brothers."

"No," Sachie said. "Romantic love. Finding that one person you can't live without."

"I'm not sure such a love exists." His lips twisted. "I think people mistake lust for love and get married only to be disappointed soon after. The new wears off, and they find themselves stuck with a person with whom they have nothing in common."

"Wow. That's defeatist," Sachie said.

"Is it?" Teller challenged. "What about you? I don't see a wedding ring."

Her lips tightened. "Like you, I never married."

"Why not?" he asked. "You're a good-looking woman."

She looked away. "I have my reasons."

"Did someone break your heart?" he asked.

She stiffened. "Yeah."

"A friend, boyfriend or family member?" he asked.

Her face paled

Teller immediately regretted putting her on the spot. "You don't have to answer that question," he said softly. "It's none of my business."

"Family member," she whispered.

He reached out and touched her hand. "I'm sorry. I should be more sensitive."

She didn't pull her hand loose from his but stared

down where they were joined. "My father. He loved me, played with me and gave me everything my heart desired. I was daddy's little girl." Sachie drew herself up, a fake smile plastered on her face. Then all the starch melted out of her. "Until I wasn't a little girl anymore. I got hips, breasts and my period. Our games stopped being fun. He did things..." Her voice broke.

Teller's heart broke for the little girl whose father had violated her trust, her love and her body. His hand tightened around hers.

A single tear slipped down Sachie's cheek. She brushed it away. "That's my sordid past. I didn't turn my father in when I should have. I didn't tell my mother, although I think she knew, but didn't want to admit it. I couldn't make him stop. Every time he came to my room, I pretended I was dead, while wishing he would die and leave me alone." Sachie snorted. "Apparently, some wishes do come true. He died of a heart attack when I was fifteen. My mother had his tombstone inscribed with the words, *Loving husband and father.* I waited until she wasn't looking and spit on it."

"Okay, you win," he said, lifting her hand to his lips. "You had a shittier childhood than I did." He pressed his lips to the backs of her knuckles. "I'm sorry for what happened to you. No child deserves that kind of physical and emotional abuse. That's why you chose a career in counseling."

She nodded. "I wanted to spare other kids from abuse at their parents' hands." Her eyebrows knitted. "I try so hard to get through to them. But, sometimes, nothing I say or do sticks, or they resent me for taking them away from an abusive family."

"The belief that it's better to stay with what you know than what you don't know…?"

"Exactly." She sighed. "Then there are the children who land in bad situations with foster care. They come out of it with no sense of belonging or belief that they can be loved."

"Like me?" He shook his head. "I'm not one of your troubled teens. You don't have to therapize me. I'm okay with how I turned out."

She cupped his cheek. "You're one of the lucky ones."

"I'm beginning to believe I am." He captured her hand, pressing his lips into her palm.

A buzzing sound captured his attention. He raised his head.

Sachie frowned and said, "Do you hear that?"

He nodded and looked around.

The sun had begun its descent toward the horizon, but there was still plenty of light in the sky.

As the sound grew louder, Teller and Sachie looked straight up.

Sunlight glinted off something shiny as it dropped down from the sky.

Teller grabbed Sachie around the waist and

yanked her off the fence rail as a drone dove toward her.

He set her on her feet and yelled, "Get down."

She dropped to her knees and covered her head and the back of her neck.

Teller ducked as the drone swept over him.

It turned, hovered and then flew low, aiming for Sachie, who hunkered close to the ground.

As the drone swerved around him, Teller cocked his leg and kicked as hard as he could, sending the drone crashing to the ground.

The buzzing stopped for a moment and then revved back up with a vengeance.

The drone had only risen several inches from the ground when Sachie lunged to her feet and performed a flying broad jump, landing in the middle of the device, crushing it into the dust.

Silence reigned, with Sachie standing like a conquering warrior on the incapacitated drone, her face set in a fierce scowl. "This ends now."

# CHAPTER 8

SACHIE RAN to the house while Teller carried the drone to the war room.

When she told Hawk, Kalea and Mr. Parkman what had happened, they abandoned the wrestling match and popcorn and hurried with her to the Brotherhood Protectors' outbuilding, Hawk on his cell phone with ranch security.

He ended the call and reported, "They'll run a search of the perimeter. Whoever was operating the drone over the ranch had to be close enough to maintain a signal."

Teller had laid the drone out on the conference table and was taking pictures of it with his cell phone.

Hawk immediately placed a video call to Hank and Swede. The two men came up in separate blocks on the screen. Hank's dark hair was wet. Swede's pale blond hair was standing on end.

"Sorry, you caught me coming out of the shower," Hank said.

"I'd just gone to sleep," Swede said. "But I'm awake now."

"What's happened?" Hank asked.

Teller explained how the drone had dropped out of the sky and attacked them. "I'm sending images of the drone and its serial number. Maybe you can trace the owner or purchaser."

"I can give it a try," Swede said.

"In the meantime, is there anything else we can do?" Hank asked. "Sachie, have you heard from your former boss about online access to patient files?"

Sachie had her cell phone out, scrolling through her emails. "There's his reply." She frowned down at the screen. "He says he can't allow it since I'm no longer an employee. However, he will allow me to come to the office and look over his shoulder as he goes through the patient data. He'll be in the office tomorrow morning." She looked up and captured Teller's gaze. "I want to catch the first flight out of here."

"No use going tonight, if he's not going to be in the office until morning."

Sachie shook her head. "I can't stay here. By coming here, I've brought my troubles with me. What if Kalea had been out there?"

"He's not after me," Kalea pointed out.

"Not yet," Sachie said. "What if he goes after people I care about to get to me?"

"You'll be fine tonight," Kalea said.

"The security detail is on high alert. They'll remain vigilant through the night," Hawk assured her.

"They didn't see the drone coming," Sachie said.

"He could be out there waiting for you to leave the ranch in the dark," Kalea argued. "It would be better if you waited until morning to head for the airport. Then at least you have a better chance of seeing the threat before he hits you broadside."

Sachie's gaze met Teller's.

"It would be better to wait until morning," Teller said. "It's already getting dark outside. If he's waiting, he has the advantage and will see us coming sooner than we'll see him."

Sachie bit down on her lip. She wanted to leave immediately, afraid that the longer she stayed, the higher the probability her stalker would find his way onto the property and hurt Kalea and her baby.

Against her better judgment, she said, "Okay. We stay one night and leave for the first flight in the morning." And if her stalker tried to hurt Kalea, Sachie would be there to stop him. She even considered sleeping outside Kalea's bedroom door.

"Now that that's settled, let me show you to your rooms," Hawk said.

With a great sense of dread, Sachie followed Hawk up the staircase to the room where he'd left her suitcase. "Teller is in the room beside yours if you need anything."

Sachie could think of something she needed from Teller, and it wasn't a glass of water or a piece of Ule's pineapple coffee cake.

The instant the thought popped into her head, she fought to shut it down. She shouldn't get used to having Teller in the same room with her twenty-four-seven. They had both been up all the previous night and needed sleep.

Sachie grimaced. What chance did she have of actually going to sleep? She hadn't had a full night's sleep since Luke's death. Every time she closed her eyes, the nightmare started.

She squared her shoulders. "I'll be fine. I think I'll get a shower and call it a night."

"It's still early," Hawk said. "You could come hang out with us in the family room."

"Thanks, but I'm tired," Sachie said. "I just want to go to bed, get up early and leave before anything else happens."

Hawk smiled. "Then good night." He pulled the door closed with Sachie inside.

She'd wanted to spend a little more time with Teller but felt it would've been awkward to say so in front of his boss. So she waited near the door, listening to the conversation between Hawk and

Teller. Then, the footsteps faded away, followed by the click of a nearby door closing.

Sachie fought the urge to throw open her door and march over to Teller's room to ask if she could visit for a while to get over her jitters. As if she wasn't already embarrassed enough. He might go running in the opposite direction or think she was a whiny baby who couldn't stand the pressure of someone stalking her, which would be true.

No. She was better off getting that shower and lying down. Having been awake for almost thirty-six hours, exhaustion should have been dragging her down.

The drone attack had spiked her adrenaline, making it really hard to settle in for the night.

Sachie sifted through her suitcase, found her best lace panties, an oversized T-shirt and a pair of shorts. She didn't understand people who slept nude. What if something happened in the middle of the night necessitating a hasty evacuation of their home? Maybe a fire or a tornado blowing the roof off. They wouldn't have time to grab clothing. They'd have to bug out in their birthday suits.

Hell, Sachie had now proven the ridiculousness of sleeping through the night nude. If she'd been nude when her home had been invaded, she might have been one of those people forced to run out into the yard as naked as the day she was born. She could imagine the look on Mrs. Henderson's face had she run over and banged on her door, begging to be let in, wearing nothing but the fear on her face.

Her lips quirking at the image in her mind and clutching her clothing to her chest, Sachie opened her door. Her panties chose that moment to slide out of her grip and drift to the floor. As she bent to retrieve them, a bigger, tanned hand beat her there.

She glanced up into Teller's face, straightening at the same time as he did.

"Headed for the shower?" he asked, laying the scrap of lace across the top of the other clothing she held.

Her heartbeat fluttered and then raced, pumping blood through her veins so fast it made her light-headed. "Yes. I am."

"Hopefully, I saved you some hot water. I was about to sit outside my room on the upper deck and thought you might like to see what it's like out here, where there's so little light pollution." He grinned. "And there's an overhang over the balcony that would make it hard for a drone to drop down on top of you."

She glanced down at her clothes.

"But you're on the way to the shower." He stepped back. "Don't let me stop you. It felt good to wash off the smell of smoke. When you're done, if you feel like it, you could join me. I'll still be out there." Teller gave her a brief nod and disappeared through the door to his room, closing it behind him.

For a moment longer, Sachie stared at the door, trying to decide whether she wanted to postpone the shower and join Teller immediately, take the shower and join him afterward, or be smart, shower and go straight to bed.

She chose to get her shower and think about options two and three while she washed away the stench of smoke from her hair and skin. After drying off, dressing and brushing the tangles from her hair, she left the bathroom and crossed the hall to her room. As she did, she glanced toward Teller's closed bedroom door, no closer to making up her mind to join him on the upper deck or going straight to bed.

Inside her bedroom, she dropped her dirty clothing in a heap next to her suitcase and walked over to the French doors that led out onto the upper deck that wrapped around the ranch house.

As he'd said he would, Teller sat in a chair, looking out at the night sky.

Before she could think too hard about the pros and cons of spending the evening stargazing with Teller, she gripped the doorknob, twisted it and stepped out on the deck, barefoot and braless beneath the oversized T-shirt.

Teller glanced her way. "I've never seen the Milky Way as clearly as tonight. Check it out."

Sachie sank into the chair beside him and stared out at the night sky filled with so many stars it looked unreal, and Teller was right. The Milky Way spread across the heavens as if someone with a giant brush had painted a swath of sparkling magic to the south. Sachie sat back and absorbed the wonder, awestruck at the brilliance of nature.

For a long time, they sat in silence. Sachie never felt awkward that they didn't say a word. The night air was decidedly cooler than earlier, making her nipples pucker. She crossed her arms over her chest, lest Teller cast a glance her way and notice the points created against the soft fabric of the T-shirt.

He didn't say anything.

Eventually, she relaxed and gave in to the peace and beauty.

"I never get tired of the skies over Hawaii," Sachie whispered.

"Did you grow up outside the light pollution?" Teller asked.

Sachie shook her head. "No. I escaped the light pollution as much as I could. I lived in a house on the side of a hill. When I couldn't handle life at home a moment longer, I'd climb the hill and drop down over the other side. I couldn't completely escape the lights, but it was much better on that side of the hill. I could see the stars and a little of the Milky Way—not like I can now, but enough to give me hope."

"Did you need hope?" he asked, his voice gentle in the darkness.

"I did," she responded. "I know exactly how Luke felt that day in my office. I swore that if I made it to adulthood, I'd do everything in my power to help kids know that they aren't alone, that things can get better."

Teller turned toward her, the light from the stars glinting off his eyes. "Like they did for you?"

She nodded and then laughed. "Well, until recently."

"We'll find the guy," Teller said.

Sachie sighed. "This view gives me hope. Witnessing something this beautiful and vast can't be a once-in-a-lifetime event. I'd like to be around to see it again."

Teller reached out a hand. "And you will."

She laid her hand in his. "Promise?"

"Damn right." He closed his fingers around hers and held her hand for another ten or fifteen minutes.

Sachie lost track of time, preferring to live in the moment. If she could, she'd stay there for the rest of the night. It beat going to bed and sinking into the nightmare sure to haunt her in her sleep.

All too soon, Teller squeezed her hand gently and said, "We should call it a night. Our flight leaves early, and I want to be there at least an hour early."

Sachie didn't express the disappointment she felt, nor the trepidation roiling in her gut at the idea of closing her eyes. She let Teller draw her to her feet and, surprisingly, into his arms.

He pressed a kiss to her forehead. "I hope you sleep well."

She lifted her face to him. "And I hope you do as well," she whispered.

He stared down into her eyes, his own dark, enigmatic pools.

Holding her close, his body pressed to hers, all he had to do was lean down a little, and he'd be close enough to kiss her. On her lips, not her forehead.

Never in her life had Sachie wished so hard for a man to claim her lips.

When he stepped away, her heart sank into her belly.

Hell, what had she expected? He was there to protect her, not kiss her.

About to duck into her room and scream her frustration into her pillow, she was stopped by strong arms coming up around her and drawing her close again.

"I want to kiss you," Teller said. "But only if you want me to."

She stared up into his face. "More than you can imagine."

He chuckled. "I can imagine a lot." His hand rose and brushed a strand of her hair back from her face. "It should be wrong to kiss you."

She raised her hands to rest against his chest. "Why? I want you to kiss me."

"You're my client," he said. "But no matter how wrong it *should* be..." he cupped the back of her neck and leaned down until his lips hovered over hers, "...it feels so right."

Her patience exceeding its limit, Sachie rose on her toes and pressed her lips to his, taking the decision out of his hands. She wanted the kiss so much that she was certain screaming into a pillow would not have been enough to ease her frustration.

But this kiss...

He started out slowly, gently exploring her mouth. When his tongue tested the seam between her lips, she opened to him, letting him past her teeth. He swept her tongue in a long, languorous caress that made her entire body tingle and then burn as her blood heated and her pulse quickened.

Sachie curled her fingers into his shirt, bringing him closer, urging him to take more. Every part of her yearned for more. She couldn't get close enough, wishing she could press her skin to his, unfettered, unblocked by the fabric separating them.

When she raised her hands to encircle the back of his neck, he lifted his head, cupped her cheek and smiled down at her in the starlight.

"We should call it a night," he said, his voice as rough as gravel. His thumb traced her lips, and he bent once more to brush his lips where his thumb had been. Then he stepped back. "Morning will be here before we know it."

Kissing this man once had only made her want to do it again.

Yet, Teller seemed content to stop at one.

"Good night, Sachie," he said.

"Good night," she managed to say.

Teller turned toward his door.

When she didn't move, he stopped, his brow dipping.

"You go on. I want to sit out here a little longer," she said.

His frown deepened. "I can't leave you out here. What if your stalker turns up?"

"Kalea and Hawk assured me the security is tight." She forced a smile. "I'll be fine. You must be exhausted. Please, don't stay up on my account."

Again, he shook his head. "I'm not going in until you do."

She glanced toward her door, her belly clenching. If she returned to her bedroom and climbed into the bed, she'd lie awake for as long as she could. But once she succumbed to exhaustion, the same dream would return, forcing her to relive the event, to stand by as her patient ended his life. She'd hear the echo of the blast, feel the splatter of blood across her face and feel the overwhelming sense of failure that weighed heavily on her heart.

"Hey," Teller touched a finger beneath her chin and turned her to face him. "Are you afraid to go to sleep?"

She lifted a shoulder and let it fall. "It's more a fear of closing my eyes. When I do, it's like my eyelids are a screen in a cinema, and the film is the same one every time."

"That day in your office?" he asked softly.

She nodded. "I haven't slept all night since. I get anxious when I think about going to bed. I know I need rest, but there's nothing restful about closing my eyes. I lay for a long time, fighting sleep, fighting the inevitable." She grimaced. "But that's not your problem. You just need me to go inside so you can." She nodded. "I'll go." When she reached for the doorknob on the French door, his hand covered hers.

"Would it help if I stayed with you?" he asked. "Maybe if you're not alone, you could sleep more peacefully."

"You'd do that? I'm pretty sure that's not part of your job description."

"No, but I know what it's like to be afraid to close your eyes, to be forced to relive, over and over, an event so horrific it steals a piece of your soul every time."

She held his gaze, noting the shadows beneath his eyes and the intensity of truth in the set of his jaw. The man had been a soldier on a Delta Force team. He'd seen violence, death and heartache. He understood what was happening to her.

"If it makes you feel better, I'll stay with you only until you go to sleep." He held up his hands. "This isn't an offer to make love. It's an offer from one friend to another. A friend who's been there."

She pulled her bottom lip between her teeth. If she had him stay with her until she went to sleep, would she actually go to sleep or lie awake wishing his offer was to make love? Then she could stay awake all night completely occupied and too busy exploring every inch of his incredible body to sink into her nightmare.

Or she could suck it up, go to bed on her own and avoid the temptation that was this Delta Force soldier who made her feel more alive than she had in... well...forever.

"Okay," she said.

"Okay, you want me to stay until you go to sleep? Or okay, get lost, don't be ridiculous, I'm a badass and can sleep on my own without some cocky son of a bitch babysitting me." He grinned.

Her lips curved upward in a smile. "Okay, I'd like for you to stay until I go to sleep. Maybe having someone with me will keep the dreams away."

"All right then," he slid a hand beneath her elbow and guided her to her door. "Let's prove the theory."

# CHAPTER 9

SACHIE PRECEDED him into the bedroom and stood awkwardly while he closed the door and secured the lock.

When he turned, he glanced around the room. "Okay. No chair, no problem." He nodded toward the bed. "You can assume the sleeping position. I can stand close or sit on the floor. Either way, I'm here for you."

Sachie pulled back the comforter, climbed into bed and settled back against the pillow. Her gaze never left Teller as he wandered around the room, pretending an interest in the paintings on the wall.

"You can't just stand there. I won't be able to sleep knowing you're unable to rest."

"Then I'll sit on the floor." He dropped down where he stood.

From where she lay on the bed, Sachie had to lean up on her elbow to see him. "I can't see you down there. You might as well not be here. Really, I'll be fine alone." She stared at him, her eyes narrowing. "Unless you want to sit on the bed. There's enough room for both of us." She moved over. "Your choice. If you're regretting your offer, don't worry about it. I've been dealing with it for the past week." She lay back against the pillow and stared up at the ceiling, prepared to keep her eyes open as long as she could.

Teller rose to his feet and stared down at her. "Anyone ever tell you that you're stubborn?"

"After many years, I've learned to be," she said, refusing to meet his gaze. "Self-preservation at its best."

Out of the corner of her eye, she could see him frown and glance down at the bed.

"Are you sure about this?" Teller asked.

"If you're going to be here until I go to sleep, yes." She tugged the comforter up to her neck. "I'm not closing my eyes until I can't hold them open a moment longer. That might take a minute."

The bed sank as Teller sat on the edge and kicked off his running shoes. He raised his legs and lay them over the comforter beneath which Sachie lay.

Even if she wanted to get closer to him, she couldn't without digging herself out from under the blanket with his body weighing it down.

Teller clasped his hands behind his neck and

leaned back against the headboard. "Do you want to talk or would you rather have silence?"

"We could talk for a while," she said. "At least until I get sleepy."

"Okay," he said. "What do you want to talk about?"

"Not our pasts," she said.

"How about our futures?" he suggested. "Where do you see yourself in five years?"

Figuring her future was a safer subject than her past, Sachie opened up about a good dream she'd always harbored. "I want to buy a house someday. Not a townhouse or condo. I want a place with a yard." She stared at the ceiling, imagining that house. "I always wanted a dog."

"What kind of dog?" Teller asked.

"A rescue. It doesn't matter how big or small. Just one that might not have had the best life. I'd like to give a dog like that a home where he'll be loved and happy for as long as he lives."

"Isn't that what we all want?" Teller mused. "To be loved and happy for as long as we live?"

"Yeah," Sachie answered softly. "Pretty much. Why is that so hard to achieve?"

Teller snorted. "I wouldn't know."

Silence stretched between them.

"What about you?" Sachie asked. "Where do you see yourself five years from now? Married, two incredibly cute kids, a house with a picket fence?"

For a long moment, Teller didn't answer.

Sachie feared she'd pushed too far with the questions. "Maybe it's time I closed my eyes and went to sleep." She forced her eyelids to close, dreading the nightmares, but feeling awful for putting Teller on the spot about his future. "I shouldn't have put words in your mouth. I'm sorry."

"Don't be," Teller's voice was warm and smooth, sliding over her like a gentle hand.

Sachie peeked at him from beneath her lowered eyelids.

He stared straight ahead, his gaze inscrutable. "I guess I've never thought that far ahead. For so long, my life was movement from one place to another, never staying long enough to set down roots or to get to know my neighbors. I didn't get attached to anyone or anywhere, knowing I might not be there tomorrow. The only attachments I've grown were with my teams. They were the only people I trusted to have my back. And I had theirs."

He didn't have to say it, but Sachie knew Teller would give his life for his brothers in arms.

"It wasn't until I came to Hawaii with my team that I even started thinking of purchasing a place of my own." He laughed. "Most guys my age have a house by now, with a wife, kids and a couple of dogs or cats. I never pictured that for myself."

"Because you didn't have that growing up?"

He nodded. "At least, not since I was ten. Maybe I didn't want to set myself up for disappointment or sorrow. I had no frame of reference other than the homes depicted on television or in the movies. But those weren't real and definitely not attainable, especially while I was on active duty. I watched my buddies marry, divorce and never get to see their kids. It wasn't for me."

She stared up at him. "And now?"

"I don't know." He sighed. "When I first came to Hawaii, I wasn't sure I'd stay. I probably wouldn't have stayed but for my friends...my team. But this place is growing on me. Being a part of the Brotherhood Protectors gives me a purpose I couldn't find in a corporate job. I can see myself actually putting down roots."

"Daring to make it your home?"

He nodded.

"Does that frighten you or at least make you itch?" she asked with a grin.

"A little," he admitted.

"Are you too conditioned to getting orders to move and feel like something will happen to send you somewhere else?" she asked.

He nodded. "I guess."

"I get that. You don't believe you can have permanence in your life, and it makes you hesitant to take a chance on anything that smells like permanence." She closed her eyes again.

"I've been in some of the worst firefights and up against some of the worst of mankind. I'm not supposed to be afraid of anything."

"Except being proven right?" She looked up into his gaze. "That nothing is permanent? I hate to break it to you, but you're right. Nothing's permanent. Sometimes, you have to take a risk and go for what you want deep down, even if you only get to have it for a short time. It's better to have some joy in life than to have none at all."

He didn't say anything for a long time.

Sachie suspected she'd bored him with her psychobabble. She closed her eyes and pretended she was finally going to sleep.

A moment later, Teller said, "You chose the right field to go into."

"I hated my childhood. I didn't want other kids to hate theirs if I could do anything to make it better." She lay her arm on the bed, her fingers brushing against his thigh. "I should've done more for Luke."

"You couldn't have known he would do what he did."

"I knew he wasn't in a good place. His whole demeanor changed over the course of a three-week period."

"You can't keep beating yourself up over it."

"I'm having a hard time letting it go. My nightmares are a continuous reminder, like I'm supposed to see something I didn't see then, learn something I can use to keep it from happening to someone else."

Teller captured her hand in his. "Going over the

event before you sleep isn't going to keep you from having a nightmare. Think of that house you'll have someday and the puppy you'll play with in the backyard."

She frowned.

"Go on," he urged. "Close your eyes and think of him. Tell me what he looks like."

She closed her eyes and tried to imagine her future puppy.

"What color is he?" Teller persisted.

"*She* is kind of a reddish-brown." Sachie was making it up, but in so doing, she could imagine a puppy that color.

"Long-haired or short-haired?"

"Long," she said.

"Must be a golden retriever...?"

"No, it's smaller than that," she said. "More like a Pomeranian with floofy long hair."

"Now, describe the yard," he said. "Is it a lush green lawn or a garden like the one at your cottage?"

Sachie spent the next few minutes dreaming up a puppy, yard and house, all with her eyes closed. Eventually, she described the inside of the house, which had a kitchen and living room with windows overlooking the ocean. By the time she got to the bedroom, she was so sleepy, she imagined climbing into bed with a smile and falling asleep beside a handsome, gentle man who spoke in warm, gentle tones that soothed rather than hurt.

. . .

TELLER SAT beside Sachie as she drifted into sleep, her hand in his, her chest rising and falling in a steady, relaxed rhythm. He closed his eyes, thinking about all that he'd learned about this amazing woman and the terrifying things that had happened to her that day. He worried that whoever was after her would somehow slip past his defenses as had almost happened with the drone.

Honolulu would present its own challenges. The city was big and chaotic, with tourists crowding the streets day and night. Protecting Sachie would be even harder there than on the Big Island.

He'd do whatever it took to keep her safe. She deserved no less. He couldn't erase the abuse of her childhood, but he could do his best to make sure she had a chance at her future.

Sometime in the midst of worrying whether he'd be enough, Teller must have fallen asleep. A muffled cry jerked him awake. He leaped from the bed, fists clenched, ready to take on the enemy.

As he searched the room in the starlight streaming through the French doors, he realized he was alone but for the woman lying in the bed behind him.

Sachie's head moved from side to side, her eyes closed, tears slipping from the corners. "No," she murmured. "Please. No."

Teller sat on the bed beside her and laid his hand on her shoulder. "Sachie. Wake up."

"No. Please don't," she whispered. "Let me help."

"Sachie, sweetheart, it's just a dream." He shook her shoulder gently. "Wake up."

She jerked and cried out and then held her breath, her entire body stiffening as if experiencing the shock of witnessing her patient's suicide all over again.

Teller couldn't stand the horror etched across her face. He had to do something to bring her out of the nightmare. Slipping his arm around her back, he gathered her close, cradled her against his body, and smoothed his hand over her hair and down her back. "It's just a dream, Sachie. You're not in your office. You're with me." His heart breaking at her distress, he pressed his lips to the top of her head. "Please, wake up."

Sachie pressed her face into his chest and sobbed.

"Oh, Sachie, it's only a dream. You're not even on Oahu. You're on the Big Island, and I've got you. "You're going to be okay," he said, repeating it over and over.

She raised her head, her eyes wet and red-rimmed, and stared at his face. When recognition dawned, the stiffness in her shoulders evaporated, and she melted into him, laying her cheek against his damp shirt. "I'm sorry," she whispered. "I'm so sorry."

"It's okay. You're okay. I'm here for you," he said, stroking her hair.

"Every time I have the dream, I know the ending, but I keep trying to reason with him," she said. "It doesn't change the outcome."

"And, sadly, it won't," Teller said.

"Why can't I dream about being attacked in the cottage or by the drone?" She laughed, the sound trailing off on a lingering sob. "At least the ending was better." She blinked up at him. "I'm sorry. You're not getting much rest. You were supposed to leave when I went to sleep."

"I'm okay. I drifted off."

"You don't have to stay. You need your sleep." She didn't move out of his arms.

She was warm and soft and fit perfectly against him. Teller had no desire to leave her. "I'm all right where I am—if you are."

She nodded. "But you can't be comfortable. At least lie down."

He scooted down the bed and lay back against the pillow, all the while holding her in his arms. When at last they were lying side by side, he gathered her close. She rolled onto her side and rested her hand and cheek against his chest. Her breath warmed his skin beneath his T-shirt.

"If all we do is lie here, it's resting our bodies," he said. "You don't have to go back to sleep if you don't want to."

"I don't," she murmured, her fingers curling into his shirt. "I'm not the least bit sleepy." Her voice trailed off, and she yawned.

"Good," he said softly. "Neither am I." Truth was that he was more awake than ever, his body fully aware of hers pressed against him. His groin tightened automatically.

"Teller?" Her voice was barely a whisper.

Teller focused on tamping down his desire to hold her even closer. The last thing she needed from him was a sexual advance. Given her past, anything between them would have to be initiated by her. And she'd have to be fully awake and aware. "Yes, ma'am?"

"You make me feel...safe..." Her words trailed off, and her breathing grew deeper.

*Safe.*

He almost laughed. She wouldn't feel so safe if she knew how much he more he wanted to do than just hold her. However, hearing her confess how she felt set him on the right path. His desire cooled.

Though he told himself he was content to just hold her, he knew it was a lie. He'd have to keep up his guard against more carnal feelings for this woman. She had enough problems without her protector becoming one of them.

While he lay with her in his arms, he directed his thoughts to the following day and what they hoped to accomplish on Oahu.

Eventually, he drifted into a fitful sleep, having his

own nightmares of an attacker getting to Sachie before Teller could reach her. He woke all the more determined to identify her stalker and take him down.

Teller's number one goal was to keep Sachie safe until they successfully neutralized the threat.

# CHAPTER 10

WHEN SACHIE WOKE to the sound of her alarm, she stretched and opened her eyes, taking a moment to remember where she was. When the memories flooded back in, she turned to the empty space beside her, wondering if falling asleep in Teller's arms had been nothing more than a delicious dream that had chased away her recurring nightmare.

She glanced around the room, the gray light of predawn giving her just enough light to verify she was alone. Her chest tightened with a longing she didn't expect. After her nightmare, she'd slept deeply. The fact she'd been held in Teller's arms had to be the reason. The good night's sleep wasn't the only reason for the unexpected and overwhelming longing she was experiencing. She'd liked being held. And not just by anybody.

Teller hadn't asked for anything, hadn't come on

to her, hadn't berated her for being scared. He'd wrapped his arms around her and held her until she woke up, and then while she finally slept.

Her body tingled at the memory of being pressed against his length.

What would it be like to lie naked with him?

Sachie flung back the covers and leaped out of bed. Such thoughts shouldn't be foremost in her mind when she had bigger problems to solve. Besides, the man was assigned to her as a protector, not a lover.

And there she was, right back to imagining them naked, writhing together in a passionate embrace. Sachie moaned, reached for jeans and a blouse from her suitcase and quickly dressed, putting an end to any ideas involving bare bodies. A quick glance at the clock on the nightstand showed she had fifteen minutes before the time they'd agreed they needed to leave.

With her hairbrush and toothbrush in hand, she left her room and crossed the hall to the bathroom. As she reached for the doorknob, the door swung open.

Teller stood before her, naked from the waist up, hair tousled and a dot of shaving cream clinging to his chin.

Sachie's breath caught in her throat, and she struggled for words, her gaze fixing on his broad chest.

"Good morning," he said, his voice low and sexy as hell, making her quiver all over.

She never quivered. What was wrong with her?

"Good morning," she managed to say.

Teller cocked an eyebrow. "Is there something you wanted, or were you going to join me in the bathroom?"

His words made her realize she was blocking his exit.

She jumped back. Heat rose up her neck and flooded her cheeks. "No. No. I'm sorry."

He shook his head. "Nothing to be sorry about." He stepped through the doorway and waved a hand. "It's all yours."

Sachie dove into the bathroom, closed the door and leaned against it. Holy shit. She'd acted as if she'd never seen a bare-chested man before.

To be honest, she'd never seen a bare-chested man like Teller.

*Get a grip, woman. He's just a man.*

Her personal experience with men hadn't been the greatest. Any attraction to this one could only lead to more heartache and disappointment.

Not that Teller was like the other men who'd let her down in the past, or at least as far as she could tell.

She straightened, relieved herself, brushed her teeth and then smoothed the tangles out of her hair. For a brief moment, she stared at her reflection in the mirror and reminded herself she was a strong, independent woman worthy of respect.

*And love.*

She'd settle for respect for now. Although she'd come a long way from the abused shell of herself that she'd been, love still seemed a stretch.

Done in the bathroom, she returned to her room, repacked her suitcase and carried it down the stairs. Leaving the case by the front door, she followed the fresh aroma of brewing coffee to the kitchen. Chef Ule stood at the stove, cracking eggs into a skillet while Teller and Hawk hovered around the coffee maker, speaking in low tones.

As she entered the room, Teller and Hawk turned.

"Ah, just in time." Hawk lifted the carafe and held it over an insulated mug. "The coffee is ready, and we were discussing a plan of action."

"Has it changed?" she asked as Hawk filled the mug and then handed it to her.

"Not at all," he said. "I'm just reminding Teller to feed any clues to Swede. He can be searching the internet while you two are pounding pavement for answers."

Sachie sipped the steaming brew carefully. "That's good to know."

"Any names you unearth or incidents you recall that might have made the news, he can research, check online articles, run background checks and, if necessary, tap into the dark web for more nefarious connections."

Sachie blinked. "He can do that?"

Hawk nodded. "He has and will when it comes to the safety of our operatives and clients."

"Kalea always sings his praises. What is he, some kind of internet hacker?" she asked.

"We prefer computer guru," Hawk said with a grin. "Can I interest you in scrambled eggs and toast? Ule should have something ready shortly."

Sachie glanced at the clock on the microwave. "Thanks for the offer, but we need to leave in the next few minutes for the airport."

"You can take the coffee with you," Hawk said.

Ule appeared beside them and held out what looked like paper lunch bags. "Ham, egg and cheese breakfast burritos and blueberry muffins. Don't go away hungry."

Sachie took the bag and hugged Ule. "Thank you, Ule."

Teller accepted his bag and shook Ule's hand. "Thanks, Ule. Your culinary skills never fail to impress." He turned to Hawk. "Thanks for putting us up for the night. We'll keep you informed of our progress."

"If you need backup, don't hesitate to call," Hawk reminded him. "With some of the team on Oahu, we can have them where you need them quickly."

"I have their numbers." Teller glanced toward Sachie. "Ready?"

She nodded and led the way out of the kitchen to the front door.

"Wait!" a voice called out.

Sachie turned back.

Kalea made her way down the stairs, holding onto the rail. By the time she reached the ground floor, she was shaking her head. "You don't realize how critical it is to see your feet when descending stairs until you can't see your feet." She grimaced. "I just want a hug before you head back to Oahu. I'm sorry the Big Island wasn't the haven you hoped. I hope you consider coming back after you nail the bastard who's doing this to you."

Sachie hugged Kalea. "I'm coming back. There are enough young people on the Big Island who need help to keep me busy, and I kind of like the smaller city and quieter pace."

"Oh, good," Kalea said. "I'd love to see you more often, and I want our baby to get to know and love Auntie Sachie as much as we do."

"I'll be back," Sachie repeated. "I want to know your baby as well. I've always wanted to be someone's Auntie."

Sachie followed Teller out the front door and down the steps to their vehicle. He opened the passenger door and held her coffee and breakfast bag as she climbed in and buckled her seatbelt.

Sachie settled the travel mugs of coffee in the cup holders and took the bags of Chef Ule's breakfast while Teller rounded the hood and slid into the driver's seat.

They sipped coffee and ate burritos during the hour-long drive across the island to Kona International Airport, only speaking to comment on the fog in the mountains and the difference in terrain and lush vegetation between the east side of the island and the rugged lava fields of the west.

Though the burrito was amazing, Sachie only ate half of hers, wrapping the rest to eat later when her stomach wasn't knotted.

"Are you nervous about flying?" Teller asked as they neared the airport.

Sachie sighed. "I shouldn't be, considering how short the flights are. We're barely up in the air before we're descending to land. I just think of all the things that could go wrong and that I have no control over. I'm in awe of Kalea's ability to fly airplanes. I don't think I could."

"I spent so much time in military aircraft, I had to learn to be okay with it," Teller said. "Mostly helicopters, flying in and out of hot zones."

"I'm sure you were more concerned about the mission ahead or the enemy shooting you down than the actual flight." Her lips twisted. "Which makes me feel like a big baby being afraid of flying from one island to another; it's like riding a bus."

"Some fears can't be explained away," Teller said. "I don't think you're a baby. I especially didn't think you were anything but a badass when you flew out of the closet ready to gut me with a butcher knife. That was pretty ballsy."

Her brow furrowed. "I almost killed you."

"*Almost* being the keyword. You did good." Teller nodded. "Had the attacker gotten to you before I did, you might have inflicted serious harm on him. He might have reconsidered any further attacks."

"Or he could've killed me, and you and I wouldn't be flying to Oahu looking for him," Sachie said, her tone flat.

Teller cast a frown her way. "Now that's just negative talk."

She sighed. "You're right. Project your desired outcome and follow through. That's how I made it through college after all that happened to me." She squared her shoulders and sat up straighter. "We're going to find who's stalking me, put him away and get on with my plan to own a house with a yard and a puppy."

"That's my girl," Teller said with a grin. "Badass to the core."

"That's me," she said, feeling anything but badass. "A firm believer in faking it until you feel it."

Forty minutes later, as the airplane left the runway and flew out over the open ocean, Sachie gladly accepted Teller's hand to squeeze throughout the flight and the landing at the Honolulu International Airport. As the plane taxied to a stop, she released her death grip on his fingers and breathed for the first time in what felt like an eternity.

She'd survived the flight from the Big Island to Oahu, placing her one step closer to finding the man who was responsible for smashing the windshield on the SUV her friend had loaned her, breaking into her cottage and burning down her office. Suddenly, the flight over seemed to be the easiest part of her quest. Maybe she'd be better off staying on the plane for the return flight to the Big Island.

As the aircraft came to a halt, she reminded herself she was worthy and didn't deserve to be terrorized by anyone. Not her father and not some cowardly stalker. It was time to take charge of her own outcome.

First stop...her old office. A patient in those files had to leap out as a potential suspect, and she was going to find him.

Okay, so the first stop wasn't her old office. It was the car rental counter. They had to get around while they were in Honolulu. Teller rented a nondescript silver four-door sedan and helped her into the passenger seat. He then folded his tall frame behind the steering wheel and adjusted the seat backward to allow his legs to fit comfortably in the confined space.

Sachie called her old boss, Dr. Janek, letting him know they were on their way. He assured them he was at the office and would be happy to let her "look over his shoulder" at the online files once she got there. His receptionist was out sick, so it would be just him.

Sachie arrived fifteen minutes later and spent thirty minutes with Dr. Janek scrolling through the files listed on the computer, asking if this patient rang any bells or that patient had anger issues, while Teller waited in the lobby. She'd have him stop, open a file to allow her to read notes to help her remember what had happened during their sessions. They'd only made it through a third of the folders before Dr. Janek had a patient consultation and had to leave. Once the doctor left to meet with his patient in the consultation room, Sachie went back to work, reviewing patient records. She focused on those she'd spent more time with than Dr. Janek had. Since he hadn't been followed, attacked or had his office burned to the ground, Sachie had to believe she was the sole target.

Teller entered the office and stood near the door. "How's it going?"

"Slow," Sachie admitted. "Nothing is jumping out or screaming, this is the one."

"Keep looking, you could be close."

She nodded and kept going, working through the

folders as fast as she dared while the psychologist was otherwise occupied with his patient.

Sachie had made it to the records of patients whose last names began with the letter S before she found the fairly recent case of Lily Franklin, a seven-year-old girl she'd removed from a home where the mother's boyfriend had abused the child. He'd used his cigarettes to burn the girl's torso and back, not once or twice, but a dozen times, while her mother was passed out on methamphetamines. A discerning teacher who'd had playground duty noticed the burns when the child had hung upside down on the monkey bars. She'd immediately rushed the girl to the nurse's office and called the police.

Sachie had been called in on the case to formally recommend the girl be removed from the home and placed in foster care, her mother, Candice Franklin, charged with neglect and the boyfriend with assault.

The mother had screamed at the police officers as they'd arrested the boyfriend and taken him to jail. She'd screamed at Sachie when she'd led the little girl away, threatening to kill her for ruining her life, never mind that the daughter's life would be forever scarred, both physically and emotionally.

Sachie grabbed a pad of paper and a pen from the doctor's desk and jotted down the patient's name, the mother's address and phone number, and the name and number of the child protective services repre-sentative who'd taken the child.

She moved on to the next file and then the next. When she reached Luke Stevenson's file, her hand shook on the mouse as she stared at the screen. For a long moment, her hand froze. She couldn't bring herself to open it.

Suddenly, Sachie was standing there again, frozen in horror. After Luke had pulled the trigger, everything had blurred in her memory. She didn't remember calling the police, though she had. Her memories were chaotic, with the blast of the fatal shot still ringing in her ears as first responders converged on the office. She'd been led out into the parking lot where colored lights strobed in the darkening sky, making her head spin.

As she stood over the monitor, her hand on the mouse, her ears rang and her head spun much like they had that day. Her vision blurred, darkening.

"Sachie?" a voice said close to her ear, penetrating the ringing sound. A hand cupped her elbow. "Are you okay?"

She looked up into Teller's handsome, stoic face as he pressed her gently onto the desk chair.

"Do you want me to take that?" he asked, indicating the mouse.

After a moment, grounding herself in his gaze, she shook her head. "No. I'm all right." Slowly, she clicked on the file icon and the folder opened, displaying information about Luke Stevenson, listing the dates he'd met with her over the past months. The final entry bore Dr. Janek's initials. He must have made the entries when Sachie hadn't been able to bring herself to return to the office, and there was an attachment on that entry. She opened the attachment to find a photocopy of a death certificate dated that day that had changed her life. To her, it was proof positive that Luke was truly dead. The faces she'd seen on the crowded streets of Honolulu and the one in the window of her cottage on the Big Island couldn't possibly have been Luke Stevenson. He was dead.

Teller rested a hand on her shoulder. "Do you know if his foster family blamed you for his death?" he asked.

Sachie lifted her shoulders and let them drop. Hell, she blamed herself for his death. Why wouldn't they?

His hand squeezed her shoulder lightly. "Do you have their names and address in his file?"

She nodded and clicked on the screen with Luke's personal information.

Teller took the pen from the desk and scrawled the information on the pad beneath Lily's data. "Do you need anything else from this file? Are there notes indicating the name of the police officer who responded to your call? Maybe he remembers something you might not have noticed."

She went back to Dr. Janek's notes and shook her head. "There's no mention of the responding officer. We can ask at the police station. They would have records."

"In the meantime, keep looking," Teller encouraged.

She worked her way through the Ts and thought she'd pretty much exhausted the files until she reached Aidan Williams, a four-year-old she'd been called in to evaluate when he'd ended up in the ER after his father had beaten him with a leather belt and dislocated his arm. The mother had disappeared months earlier, having returned to the contiguous forty-eight states, leaving the father to deal with a four-year-old.

At the court hearing, the father had blamed the kid for misbehaving and had blamed Sachie for taking the boy from him and sending him to jail. He'd sworn he'd get even. That had been over a year ago. The father had been sentenced to two years. Could he have been released?

Sachie wrote down his name and moved on, finishing her search through the Zs.

She peeled the notes off the pad, pushed back from the computer and stood as Dr. Janek appeared in the doorway. "Ready to continue your search?" he asked.

Sachie smiled at her former boss. "No. I think I have what I need."

"Well, let me know if you need anything else. I hate that you're having to go through this on the heels of what happened."

She snorted. "You and me both. I just hope whoever it is doesn't come after you next."

"I'm already looking over my shoulder," Dr. Janek said. "If you decide to stay on Oahu, you're always welcome to come back to work here. It's not the same without you."

"Thank you. It's nice to know I was appreciated." She hugged the doctor and headed for the door.

Teller followed.

Once outside, he pulled out his cell phone. "Let me send a picture of those names and addresses to Swede so he can start fishing."

She held up the handwritten notes while Teller snapped pictures of them. He sent them via text to the Brotherhood Protector hacker.

Sachie hoped he found something.

Teller pocketed his cell phone. "Where next?"

"The police station," she said. "I want to see if they've made any headway on finding whoever broke into my apartment and drowned my pillows. I also need to let them know what happened on the Big Island, in case they hadn't heard. There's a chance they might know if some of the people on our list have had further encounters with the law."

Teller nodded. "Then what?"

Sachie shook her head. "I'd really like to know

what bothered Luke so much that he thought his only way out was to end his life."

"I thought you said he'd hurt his girl."

"That's just it. He never hit her. He grabbed her to keep her from doing something he was against. When she pulled free, she fell and hit her head against a wall. Though he didn't actually hit her, he blamed himself. He was afraid he was genetically predisposed to abuse and would turn out to be abusive like his father."

"Sounds like he had a couple of things going on that pushed him over the edge," Teller said.

Sachie's lips pressed together. "Anyway, I want to talk with his foster family to see if they noticed him acting strangely or if they'd had a fight. They might also have an idea who Luke was hanging out with. I'd like to speak with his friends and Kylie, his girlfriend. Maybe that will help me understand the signs I should've looked for, so I can figure out ways to de-escalate situations like that if I'm ever in a similar scenario. I never want another kid to die that I could've helped."

"I know you're still hurting from Luke's suicide, and I agree with learning from tragedy to avoid it happening again." Teller gripped her arms and stared down into her eyes. "I'm on board with all of that...as long as we stay on course to find your stalker before he strikes again."

Sachie met his gaze and held it with determination and purpose swelling inside. She'd be damned if she let anyone control ever her again. "Damn right. Let's find that stalker."

# CHAPTER 11

TELLER DIDN'T HAVE any problem chasing down answers as to why a teen had felt so trapped he'd committed suicide, but only after they found the person bent on terrorizing Sachie. Whoever it was must have known about the teen's suicide and was tapping into her inevitable nightmares to scare her even more.

But why?

He hoped to get the answers soon. With Swede working the internet, he might be able to learn more about the people who'd publicly threatened Sachie at some point. But while they waited for word from him, they'd do some of their own sleuthing.

Sachie gave him directions to the Hawaii Police Department.

When they walked in, she asked to see Detective Mahalawai. The desk sergeant made a call. Moments later, they were shown into the inner sanctum of the department, weaving between desks to an office in the corner.

Though the door was closed, Sachie knocked on the doorframe.

A man in uniform swiveled in his desk chair and glanced up. "Sachie, come in, come in." He rose and greeted her with a hug. "How are you?" His brow furrowed as he stared down at Sachie.

"I'm okay," she said.

Teller wanted to tell the man that was a lie. She was being stalked and had almost been killed. In Teller's books, that wasn't okay. But he held his tongue. This was her sandbox, and people she knew and had worked with.

Sachie turned to Teller. "Jim, this is Teller Osgood. He works with the Brotherhood Protectors, an organization based on the Big Island. He's prior service Army Delta Force, and he's helping me with an investigation."

"I've heard of them, but you're the first one I've met." He held out his hand to Teller. "Nice to meet you and thank you for your service."

"Nice to meet you," Teller said..

After the detective released Teller's hand, he turned back to Sachie. "I'd heard you'd moved to the Big Island. What brings you back so soon?"

"The same reason I left," she responded. "I thought I'd get away from whoever broke into my apartment in Honolulu by moving to the Big Island."

Jim's lips thinned. "Didn't work, did it?"

"I don't know if you get the reports from Hilo, but someone broke into my house the night before last. He was armed and fired at least three rounds."

"Damn, Sachie." The detective ran his gaze over her. "Are you all right? You weren't hit, were you?"

She shook her head. "No, but Teller was while protecting me."

Detective Mahalawai's eyes rounded, his glance shifting to Teller.

Teller raised a hand. "Only a flesh wound."

"Did you get a look at the perpetrator. Could you identify him?"

Sachie shook her head again. "No. And he didn't stop at breaking into my house. My office in Hilo burned to the ground in the early hours of yesterday morning, and I was attacked by a drone while staying with a friend at Parkman Ranch. I need to find out who's doing this and end it."

The detective nodded. "Were they able to lift prints? Were any clues or messages left behind on any of those attacks?"

"No prints, just like at my apartment here. But yes, on messages. I had a voicemail on my cell phone from an Unknown number stating, *You failed me. Now you will pay.* And *You Failed Me* keyed into the side of Teller's SUV while we were dealing with the fire."

"Have you done anything to anyone lately that would make them want to hurt you?" His lips twisted. "I'm sure there's a long list of angry parents when you removed their children from their abusive homes. I'll need names. And what about the kid who committed suicide? Did he have family or friends who might blame you? I'll need their names as well. Have you had a breakup with an obsessive boyfriend who might be angry at being dumped?"

Sachie snorted. "No, on the boyfriend." She handed the detective the names of the two people she'd noted from Dr. Janek's patient database. "These two were parents of small children who'd been physically abused and moved into child protective services. They each swore they would get me."

"But the message stating *You Failed Me* sounds more personal," the detective said. "It's more personal, like from someone you were counseling who didn't benefit from your work with them."

Sachie's brow furrowed.

Teller could almost guess who Sachie thought of first. She didn't need someone to tell her she'd failed Luke. But he was dead. He couldn't be sending those messages. If the harassment was revenge for allowing Luke to go through with the suicide, they had to find someone who had cared enough about the teen to blame the last person who saw him alive for allowing him to successfully kill himself.

All the more reason to dig into Luke's family and friends.

Teller's cell phone vibrated in his pocket.

While Sachie briefed the detective on her reasons for pulling the names she had, Teller checked his text messages.

Swede had already gotten a hit on those names Teller had given him.

When Teller clicked on the link, he landed on a video of a woman screaming in a courtroom as a man was led out in a prison uniform and handcuffs. The man glared at the woman and glanced over his shoulder at someone else, who was out of range of the camera. He shouted something that sounded like, *I'll make you pay for this.*

The woman, her hair in disarray, dark circles under her eyes, her face pale and gaunt like those poor souls who were strung out on drugs, screamed at the judge until he slammed down his gavel and called for order. She had to be forcibly removed from the courtroom by the bailiff. The article accompanying the video clip reported that the man, Travis Finkel, had been sentenced to two years in prison for child abuse. The woman, Candice Franklin, had her child officially remanded into the custody of Child Protective Services, as Ms. Franklin had been accused of neglect and endangering her child. She'd been determined unfit to care for the girl. The report was dated six months ago.

A moment later, another link appeared in a text message from Swede.

It was a link to a news article from a Hawaiian online news source, reporting the same woman, Candice Franklin, had been rushed to the hospital after her boyfriend, fresh out of prison after only serving six months of a two-year sentence for child abuse, had violated his parole, brutally attacked her and then disappeared. The police had issued an All-Points Bulletin for Travis Finkel, warning the public he was dangerous. The article was dated two weeks ago—around the same time Luke had shot himself and Sachie's troubles had begun.

A man fresh out of prison might be interested in dishing out some payback for the ones responsible for putting him there, especially if he'd promised to do just that during his hearing.

Swede also sent the name, address and phone number of Finkel's parole officer and the man's grandmother, who lived on the opposite side of the island.

"We'll check into these people," the detective said.

Teller glanced up. "My contact says Travis Finkel was released from prison two weeks ago and has since put Candice Franklin in the hospital. You'll have to find him before you can ask if he's the one who has been targeting Ms. Moore because he's since disappeared."

The detective frowned. "I hadn't heard, but I'll be sure to let you know when we find him."

Teller's eyes narrowed. "Hopefully, before he finds Ms. Moore."

Detective Mahalawai looked from Teller to Sachie. "Will you two be staying on Oahu?"

Sachie's gaze met Teller's. "We'll be here until we determine who's stalking me."

Teller added, "And put a stop to his terror campaign against Ms. Moore."

Mahalawai nodded. "I take it you'll be looking into the potential suspects as well?"

Teller nodded.

"I'll let you know what we find," the detective said. "Please keep us informed on anything you uncover or names of other people you might suspect."

"We will." Sachie slipped her hand into the crook of Teller's elbow. "Thank you for your time, Detective Mahalawai."

Teller led Sachie back through the maze of desks to the exit.

Before they reached the exit, a police officer waved at them from across the room. "Sachie Moore, is that you?"

Sachie smiled and waited while the man made his way toward them. "Officer Roland, it's been a while, hasn't it?"

"Yes, it has." He shook her hand. "What was it?

The case with the teen runaway who was reported missing?"

She nodded. "I think that was the one. What was it, almost two years ago?"

Roland nodded. "It's good to see you. Are you still consulting for the Child Protective Services?"

Sachie shook her head. "No. I moved to another island. I'm only on Oahu for a brief stay."

"I'm sorry to hear that. I'm sure they miss you with all the work you did helping get kids out of bad situations."

The officer frowned. "Did your move have anything to do with the teen who committed suicide?" The man shook his head. "That had to have been a traumatic experience."

Sachie nodded, but didn't respond.

"What makes a kid do something like that?" the officer asked. "Did he tell you what was bothering him?"

"He was a troubled you man. I thought he was on his way to getting his life together and then—" she waved her hand. "I was shocked."

Roland touched her arm. "I'm sure you were. I'm sorry that happened to you."

"I'm sorry it happened to him." Sachie gave the officer a stiff smile. "I need to go. It was good to see you again."

She turned and hurried toward the exit.

Once they were in the rental car, Teller reached

across the console and took her hand without saying a word.

She didn't pull free but covered both of their hands with her other hand. She sat staring at them for a long moment. "I guess I'm still too close to what happened. I'm fine one minute and a complete basket case seconds later." She looked up with a weak smile. "But I didn't come here to indulge in uncontrolled weeping. I came to find the bastard who won't leave me the hell alone."

With each word she spoke, she straightened a little more until she sat up with her shoulders back and chin held high.

She'd been through so much, and yet she wanted to see this quest through, even if it put her life in danger. The woman had guts.

Teller admired that in her. He squeezed her hand gently and pulled his free, placing it on the steering wheel.

Before he could ask where they were going next, his cell phone vibrated in his pocket. He dug it out and checked the sender. "It's Swede again," he said. "He looked up Scott Williams, expecting to find him in Hawaii's main prison, the Halawa Correctional Facility. He wasn't there. He was released over a month ago after serving half of his sentence and completing behavioral counseling to learn to control his anger. He's living in a halfway house. Swede sent the address." He glanced up from his cell phone. "Do you want to let the detective know about Williams?"

"Yes," Sachie said. "But maybe not until we have a chance to check him out first."

Teller shifted into reverse and backed out of the parking space in front of the station. "So, we're going to the halfway house first?"

Sachie nodded. "We don't have to confront the man. We could ask the house manager if any of the residents broke curfew the night before last. If they can prove Williams was here during that time, it takes him out of the suspect pool."

Playing devil's advocate, Teller pointed out, "For doing the job himself. What if he hired someone else to follow you to the Big Island?"

Sachie's lips twisted. "That would be harder to prove." Her eyes narrowed, and she touched a finger to her chin. "We could ask for his phone number. You said your guy, Swede, can tap into databases. Can he tap into his cell phone provider's database and see the numbers coming in or going out, or track where he's going or where he's been?"

Teller's brow dipped. "I'm not sure. But remember, we're not cops. The house manager might not be willing to divulge that kind of personal information about a resident."

"I can claim I've been assigned as his court-ordered counselor, and I want to get ahead of our sessions."

"I'd think the court-ordered counselor would already have his number."

She lifted her shoulders. "I don't know. We can come up with something."

"I'm not trying to be negative. I just want us to be prepared for pushback."

"We're here on Oahu, and we need to start somewhere." Her chin set in a stubborn line. "Let's get there and see what we're up against."

Teller nodded. "Yes, ma'am."

Using the map application on his cell phone, he drove through the city streets, heading away from the tourist-crowded areas of Honolulu into the hills where the full-time residents who worked the resorts and businesses lived. In an older neighborhood with homes that probably dated back to the sixties and seventies, the directions brought them to their destination in front of a two-story house, the wood siding thick with many coats of paint, the steps up to the front porch worn in the middle.

Teller had to park a block away, as the house didn't have a garage or carport, much less a driveway.

Sachie pulled her hair back, securing it in a tight ponytail at the nape of her neck, and slipped on a pair of sunglasses. "Ready?"

Teller gave her a mock salute. "I'm ready, detective."

Her lips twisted. "If we happen to run into Mr.

Williams, I'd rather he didn't recognize me immediately."

"I'm sure he won't. You look like one of those real housewives of whatever city they're in now, not the mild-mannered counselor who ruined an abusive father's life."

"Shut up," she said, her lips quirking on the corners. "Let's get this over with." Wiping the smile off her face, she pushed open her door and stepped out onto the sidewalk.

Teller met her at the back of the sedan and walked with her to the halfway house. He didn't knock. Instead, he twisted the doorknob and pushed the door open. Taking the lead, he went in first.

"Can I help you?" a male voice called out through the open door to the left.

"We hope so," he answered and waited for Sachie to step in beside him.

She breezed past him with a friendly smile on her face, her hand held out to the man seated at a desk in what might once have been a sitting room. "Good morning, Mr...." She tipped her sunglasses downward and stared around the room as though looking for a nameplate.

"Mike Foster." The man rose to his feet and shook her hand. "What can I do for you?"

Sachie shot a brief smile toward Teller. "I could tell you that I'm a representative of the federal prison regulatory board here to conduct a survey of halfway houses and their residents as part of a statewide effort to ensure our federal tax dollars are being spent wisely, but that would be a lie."

Foster crossed his arms over his chest. "Strange way to start a conversation."

"I know." She took off her sunglasses and sighed. "It's not in my nature to lie. It is, however, in my nature to get answers—especially when my life depends on it. I'm Sachie Moore. I've consulted with the Hawaii Police Department and Child Protective Services. One of my cases was a child beaten by his father...one of your residents recently released from prison. In the past couple of weeks, I've had my apartment broken into here in Honolulu, my cottage broken into when I moved to the Big Island and my new office there burned to the ground. I've received threats and even been attacked by a drone. I need to know who's doing this and stop him."

"And you think it might be one of our residents?" Foster motioned toward a chair. "Have a seat." He waited until she sank into the chair before he settled into his seat behind the desk.

"I'm going through cases that ended up in court where the abusers' parting words were a threat to me. Scott Williams was one of those. He was released recently, and I have to start somewhere."

"What do you need to know?" Foster asked.

"Has he broken curfew in the past two weeks?" Teller asked.

"Mr. Williams works at a meat-packing plant. Either I or the other house manager is in contact with his supervisor to make sure he arrives on time and confirm what time he leaves the facility. He goes to work early in the morning and is off by noon. It's not the usual arrangement for our residents to work an irregular shift like that, but it can be hard to place them in gainful employment with a felony record."

"I can understand," Sachie said.

"We know how long it should take for him to get to the facility, wait for a text from his supervisor when he arrives and record those times. He gets to work on time and gets back to the house on time unless he calls ahead to inform us that he's going for a haircut or to the grocery store, which he will be doing today."

"Did he work yesterday morning?" Sachie asked.

Foster ran his fingers across a computer keyboard and stared at the monitor. "No. He was off work that day."

She frowned. "Was he here at the house during that time?"

The manager's brow dipped in concentration. "Our records indicate he never left the house."

"Did you or one of the other managers actually see him at all yesterday?" Teller asked.

Foster shook his head. "I wasn't on duty yesterday. I could call my counterpart and ask if he has laid eyes on Williams. But he would've noted when he left and came in, if he actually left the building. There's only one door they can use to enter or leave the house. The other is locked twenty-four-seven."

"Is there always someone at this desk?" Teller asked.

Foster nodded. "Yes."

"What about bathroom or smoking breaks?"

"Well, we make exceptions for those. We aren't meant to be a prison, but rather a transition from prison to regular life." Foster leaned his elbows on the desk. "Look, I've only had a few conversations with Scott since he arrived. His records indicate he's sober now and plans to stay that way. He also said he regrets what he did to his kid. He told me he's going to work hard to prove to the court he can be a good parent so he can regain custody of the boy."

"I really hope he is turning his life around," Sachie said. "So many children would rather go back to a parent they know than to be passed around in the foster care system, even if they suffered some kind of abuse with that parent."

"You say Mr. Williams is at work today?" Teller asked. "Did you record what time he left to go?"

Foster shook his head. "No. Bryan was on that shift. He would've made the entry." He stared at the computer monitor, a frown denting his forehead. "Unfortunately, he didn't record it this morning. I don't know why I didn't see that. Nor did he record the supervisor's text."

Teller tensed.

"I got here an hour ago and did get a call from Williams telling me he had an errand to run after he left work today, so he'd be later getting back than usual. Hold on." Foster picked up his cell phone and placed a call. For a long moment, he listened without saying anything. "Bryan's not answering. That's not unusual. He's probably sleeping since he had the night shift." He placed another call. "Hello, this is Mike Foster. Is Scott Williams at work today? He is? Do you know what time he clocked in?" His brow furrowed. "Doesn't he usually report in at four a.m.? I see." He nodded. "No. I don't need to speak to him. Just checking in. Thank you." He ended the call. "Apparently, Williams wasn't scheduled to work today but got called to fill in for someone who was going to be late. He arrived at eight and should get off at noon. I can't explain why it wasn't recorded, but he is at the plant now."

"What plant is that?" Sachie asked.

"The one in Kapolei," Foster said. "Are you going to pay him a visit out there?"

Sachie's brow wrinkled. "Maybe. I'd like to ask him some questions, but I don't want to get him in trouble with his boss. Does he take public transport, or does he drive his own vehicle?"

"A friend of his kept his car while he was in prison. It's a gray sedan with a sticker of a turtle on the back windshield."

Sachie rose from the chair and extended her hand. "Thank you for everything."

"I hope you find the guy causing you problems," he said and grimaced. "And I hope it's not Williams. He seemed sincere about wanting to get his son back."

"I hope it isn't him as well," Sachie said.

She led the way out of the house.

Teller pulled the door closed and descended the porch steps with Sachie.

She glanced back at the house and then ducked between the house and the one beside it.

"Where are you going?" Teller asked, hurrying to catch up.

"I just wanted to check something out." She walked around the two-story building, her eyes narrowed as she looked at the house from every angle, making a complete circle around it.

Teller studied it as well. Nothing stood out until they rounded the other side, where a metal fire escape clung to the siding near the far corner next to a window.

"Think he might have slipped out a window and down the fire escape?" Teller studied the rusty metal. "Doesn't look very sturdy."

She shrugged. "It's a possibility."

Once they were back in the rental car, Teller asked. "Where now?"

"Kapolei," she said. "It's on the other side of the airport from here."

"Do you think he could've left the house unde- tected and had enough time to fly to the Big Island, do everything he did and still get back in time to go to work at eight in the morning?

"There are early flights from Hilo that could get him back in time," she said. "And if he was home by noon the day before my cottage was broken into, he could've been on the Big Island the entire time, and the people at the halfway house wouldn't have been any the wiser—seeing as they had no record of him going to work this morning."

# CHAPTER 12

TELLER DROVE out of the neighborhood and merged onto H1, heading west to Kapolei. By the time they reached the outskirts, it was nearly noon.

"What's the plan?" Teller asked. "Are we going to corner him in the parking lot and question him there?"

"Something like that," she said. "We have to get there before he gets off to do that."

They were within a block of the meat-packing facility when a gray sedan passed them going the opposite direction.

Sachie twisted in her seat and looked out the back of the sedan. "That was him. The car has a turtle on the back window."

Teller slowed, put on his left blinker and waited for a break in the oncoming traffic.

Sachie remained turned in her seat. "I can still see him, but he's about to go around a curve."

A gap appeared in the oncoming traffic. It wasn't much of one, but Teller couldn't wait any longer. He hit the accelerator and spun the steering wheel at the same time. Tires squealed as the sedan did a one-eighty, fishtailing until Teller had it headed straight ahead.

"I lost sight of him," Sachie said, leaning toward the dashboard. "He can't be too far ahead. The traffic isn't moving that fast."

The slow traffic didn't help Teller catch up. Every chance he got, he wove around a slower vehicle and sped up again, only to get trapped behind another. As they rounded the curve, Sachie squinted, searching the road ahead. "I think that's him, six cars ahead. He's merging onto H1, heading back to Honolulu."

The car in front of Teller slowed almost to a complete stop to take a right turn onto a side street. With another car passing him on the left, Teller had no choice but to slam on his brakes and wait for the driver to complete the turn. As soon as he did, Teller punched the gas, sending the rental shooting forward. Moments later, he flew onto H1, merging into traffic. With multiple lanes to choose from, he whipped around vehicles using the far-left lane and nearly passed the gray sedan as it veered to the right onto an exit ramp.

"He's getting off!" Sachie yelled at the same time

Teller had come to that conclusion. Quickly checking his rearview and side mirror, he swerved sharply, crossing three lanes of traffic and just making it to the exit to the sound of horns honking.

Ahead, William's car slowed at a green traffic light and turned left.

By the time Teller reached the light, it was red. He would have blown through it except a police car waited at the light to his right, forcing him to come to a complete halt and wait for the cross traffic to pass, along with the police car, and for his light to turn green.

Sachie sat as far forward as she could and still be secured in her seatbelt.

"Still see him?" Teller asked when the light blinked green. He pulled onto the road and fell in behind the cars slowing for the next light in a long line of traffic lights at every intersection.

Sachie craned her neck to look over the tops of the vehicles in front of them. For a long moment, she said nothing. "I think I see him. No... Yes! That's him. Second car at the fourth light in front of us."

Teller did his best to catch up, but he was stuck in the gridlock, slowly moving forward. Fortunately, the lights synchronized in his favor, and although he moved at a snail's pace, he didn't have to stop at a red light.

Soon, the traffic thinned. Only three vehicles moved between them and the gray sedan with the turtle sticker. At this point, Teller was in no hurry to close the distance. He didn't want Williams to know he was being tailed.

They'd left the busier four-lane streets and moved into a residential neighborhood with single-family homes and a park with fields for organized sports like baseball and soccer.

The last vehicle between them turned onto a side street.

Williams's gray sedan slowed in a school zone across from a park. He pulled into a parking area dedicated to the park and stopped.

"Want to stop and talk with him?" Teller asked, slowing as they approached.

"No," she said. "Drive on by, then turn onto the street flanking the park. I want to know what he's up to."

Teller drove past Williams in his parking area to turn onto the road that ran along the side of the park. "Think he's meeting someone there for nefarious purposes?"

Her lips pressed together, a frown pulling her brow low. "For all we know, he's stopping to eat a picnic lunch. It is a pretty park."

Like so many parks in the area, this one was a mix of walking paths through Banyan trees, baseball diamonds and soccer fields for children's and adults' sports leagues.

Sachie pointed ahead. "Pull into that parking area by the banyan trees."

As soon as Teller brought the car to a halt, Sachie jumped out.

Teller hurried to join her as she set off on one of the paths, meandering through the massive trees with their thick canopies of leaves and arrays of aerial roots and prop roots dangling from the branches above.

Sachie moved quickly toward the other parking area, where the gray sedan was parked.

As they neared, Teller spotted Williams seated on a bench eating a sandwich.

Teller chuckled softly. "You called it. He's having a picnic lunch in the park."

She stopped in the shadow of one of the banyans. "Why here? Why not at a park closer to the halfway house?"

A loud bell rang, drawing Teller's attention to the school across from the park, and across from where Williams sat on the park bench.

As children streamed out into the playground surrounded by a chain-link fence, the man lowered the hand with the sandwich and leaned slightly forward.

Sachie moved closer to the man on the bench. "Is he watching the children?"

Teller reached for her hand. "In case he looks this way, he will only think we're a couple walking through the park. "Do you think he chose this park because it's across from an elementary school?"

Sachie shivered. "I hope not. It's too creepy. Makes me want to call him out on it."

When she started forward, Teller held onto her hand, bringing her to a halt. "Wait."

She turned toward him and then glanced back at the playground.

A small boy chased a ball to the fence, bent to pick it up and paused. He glanced across the road as if looking for something or someone. Then, he grinned and waved.

Scott Williams waved back. He didn't leave the bench or go to talk to the little boy but kept his distance.

At the angle they stood observing the man, Teller could see his smile.

The boy waved again, turned with the ball and ran back to play with his friends.

Williams sat on the bench until the bell rang again and the children filed into the building. Recess was over.

Williams gathered his trash, tossed it into a bin and headed for his car.

"Do you want to follow him?" Teller asked, ready to sprint back to their rental.

"No. That won't be necessary," Sachie said.

Teller turned to Sachie to find tears slipping down her face. He cupped her cheeks and stared down into her watery eyes, his heart squeezing hard in his chest. "Hey, why the tears?" Hell, he could handle bullets better than a woman's tears, any day—especially this woman's.

She gave him a weak laugh. "Just when you've lost faith in humankind, something like this reminds you that not everyone is bad or out to hurt others."

Teller glanced toward the gray sedan pulling out of the parking lot. "You think it's okay for a grown man to lurk outside an elementary school playground?"

"I recognized the little boy." Sachie looked up into Teller's eyes, her own filling again. "It was Aiden Williams, Scott's son. He came to see his son."

"What about him not leaving the house for an entire day and the house manager not recording that he left?"

"It could've happened as you suggested." Sachie started moving back to where they'd parked. "Bryan might've gone on a bathroom break, not expecting anyone to leave at that hour. Williams wasn't supposed to work today, but his supervisor said he was asked to fill in for someone else." She shook her head. "I think it would've been a stretch for him to fly out to the Big Island, stir up all that trouble and get back in time to show up at work at eight."

Teller opened the passenger door and held it for Sachie to climb in.

He rounded to the other side of the car and slipped in behind the wheel. "Now where?"

"I'd like to talk with Candice Franklin if she'll see me."

SACHIE STARED at the front windshield, images of a little boy standing on the other side of a fence waving at his father etched in her mind. She really hoped Scott Williams was committed to a better life for himself and his son. Like all children, Aiden deserved to live a happy childhood with a parent who loved and protected him. She'd never liked taking children away from their parents, but she couldn't stand back and let a child be neglected or abused by those parents.

Teller checked the text Swede had sent for the address and brought it up on his map application. "Are you going to let Foster know where we found Williams?"

Sachie had rolled that question over in her mind before Teller had asked. "Though I like to think his picnic in the park is harmless, and he only wanted to see his kid, I'd hate to be wrong. So, yes. I feel like it's my responsibility to let Foster know. I'm not sure if Williams has visitation rights with Aiden or if he has been ordered to keep his distance from the boy."

The map led them back to H1 to another exit and back into a seedier neighborhood with homes that had seen better days years ago. Many had cars parked in the tiny front yards, some propped on concrete blocks, missing not only tires but their wheels as well.

If it wasn't chickens wandering the streets, it was stray dogs that barely moved off the pavement as Teller eased along the narrow streets, coming to a stop in front of a dilapidated shack that appeared to be held together by plywood and duct tape.

Sachie's heart went out to Candice Franklin. To live in such squalor was bad enough. To have an old boyfriend beat the shit out of her after being released from jail was taking it to the next level of horrible.

She got out of the car, not looking forward to stepping into this woman's house. She'd been in homes no human or animal should live in. She suspected this was one of those.

Teller walked with her up to the door and knocked.

"Go away," a voice called out from inside.

"Ms. Franklin, could we have a few minutes of your time?" Teller called out.

"I'm not buying. Ain't got no money anyway," she said and then erupted in a hacking cough. "Damn."

"Candice," Sachie called out, "we're looking for Travis and hope you can help us."

"You and everyone else," Candice called out. "That no good, son of a bitch nearly killed me." Again, more coughing.

"Please. We won't take up too much of your time," Sachie persisted.

"Door's open," the woman inside said. "Travis busted the lock."

Teller pushed the door inward and stepped through the entryway.

Sachie followed and wished she'd taken a deep breath while she'd been outside.

The place reeked of what smelled like cigarettes and rancid trash. The small house was a hoarder's nightmare, with dirty clothing littering various surfaces, old pizza boxes stacked in the corners and beer cans strewn across a carpet that had become the drop cloth of a desperate woman's life. Candice Franklin lay on an old sofa, wearing a pair of cut-off jean shorts and a faded and torn AC/DC T-shirt. One arm was draped over her eyes, the other in a cast and a sling across her belly. "What do you want? I already told the police I don't know where that loser went. They should never have let him out of jail."

When Candice lowered her arm, Sachie swallowed hard to keep from gasping.

Her narrow face was bright shades of purple and blue, with one eye swelled shut, her lip swollen to twice what would have been normal and a scabbed gash on her left cheek that would leave an ugly scar.

She must have seen the horror in Sachie's expression because she snorted and said, "Travis likes to leave his calling card. Don't you think I'm pretty?"

She tried to smile, managing only to lift one side of her mouth, making it more of a sneer.

"I'm sorry this happened to you," Sachie said. "We'd like to see him hauled back to jail. Did he say anything about where he was heading?"

"You think I wouldn't have told the police already? I want him back in prison even more. He blamed me for putting him there in the first place, when it was what he did to my sweet Lily that got him arrested. He blamed me and that woman working with the police who stood up in court and testified against him."

Candice squinted through her semi-good eye. "I know you, don't I?" She squinted again. "I never forget a face. Names now are a different story. Were you one of the nurses at the hospital when they brought me in after Travis tried to remodel my face and ribs?"

Sachie shook her head. "No, ma'am." She didn't want to remind the woman that she was the one who had testified in court against Travis and Candice. They needed any information the battered woman could give them that might help them find Travis. "You say you don't know where Travis went, but before he went to prison, did he have places he liked to go to get away from it all? Maybe to a family member or friend's house? Doesn't he have a grandmother who lives on the island?"

Candice snorted. "She won't have nothing to do

with his sorry ass. Last time he visited her, he stole the money she had hidden under her mattress. If he'd asked for it, she probably would've given it to him. She practically raised him after his mother went off with a younger man and didn't want a kid tagging along. When Travis stole the money from his grandma's stash, she cut him off. Told him she didn't want to see him anymore. He won't have gone there."

"Friends?"

"He had some friends in that motorcycle gang. They wanted him to join, but he didn't have a motorcycle. I'm not sure where they live, but they hang out at that dive of a bar—the Leather and Chains. If he ain't with them, he might be hiding out on the other side of the island with his cousin, Reuben Jones, on the North Shore. He works on surfboards during the day and deals drugs when he needs extra income. You didn't hear that from me. Never did like Reuben. That horse's ass punched his girl in the gut while she was pregnant with his kid. Made her miscarry. Probably just as well. They didn't need to bring a brat into that environment. He and Travis are sadistic bastards. Don't care who they hurt, young or old."

Candice closed her eyes and laid her good arm over her face. "Why was it you wanted to talk to Travis?"

"We think he might be involved in other attacks," Sachie said, "and want to stop him before he hurts anyone else."

"Shouldn't the cops be doing that?" Candice said to the ceiling. "Frankly, I don't give a rat's ass. Travis can rot in hell for all I care. Just keep him away from me." She opened her eyes again and stared at Sachie. "I know you from somewhere, just can't put my finger on it."

"I'm sure it will come to you." Sachie glanced around the small living area. "Can I get you anything?"

"A water bottle from the fridge would be great and save me from trying to get up to get it." She coughed and held her ribs at the same time. "Dammit. That hurts."

Sachie picked her way across the debris to the refrigerator, snagged a half-empty water bottle from the door and returned to Candice. "I hope you get well soon."

"Thanks," she said and scooted into a sitting position. "What did you say your names were?"

"Teller Osgood," Teller said.

Sachie didn't add her name to his announcement and wouldn't unless Candice demanded her name. There was no use upsetting the woman further by letting her know Sachie had been involved in removing her daughter, Lily, from her home.

"The motorcycle gang and his cousin Reuben?" Sachie prompted. "Are those the only people or places he might go to?"

"Yeah. Now, if you don't mind, I'm done talking. Leave."

Sachie turned, met Teller's gaze and lifted her chin toward the door. "Ready?"

"Yes, ma'am," he said and led the way out of the shack and down the stairs to the sidewalk.

Back in the car, Sachie sighed. "I guess you know where I want to go next?"

"If it's to the motorcycle club bar, you're crazy," he said. "But I won't say no, though I might have my team on standby."

"Travis sounds like he hasn't learned how to control his anger during his brief time in prison. We might need to call in reinforcements."

# CHAPTER 13

TELLER WASN'T THRILLED about busting into a biker bar looking for one of their own. And he sure as hell didn't want to take Sachie in there with him.

Yet, he knew if he didn't take her, she'd find her own way there. What chance did a lone female counselor have against a rabid gang of bikers who might be either drunk or high on illicit drugs...or both?

"You know bikers don't necessarily hang out all day at their favorite bar. They're like vampires and come out at night," Teller said.

Sachie cocked an eyebrow and stared across the console at Teller. "And you know this because you've frequented biker bars?"

"Not necessarily," he said. "However, going in looking like a highly educated cream puff will flag you before you even cross the threshold."

Sachie's lips twitched. "What are you saying? I need to look more like a badass than a cream puff?"

"Actually, yes." He cast a glance her way as they drove away from Candice's sad house in the middle of an equally sad neighborhood of homes with peeling paint and sagging roofs. Even the houses looked like they'd lost hope. He hadn't liked the smell of Candice's home, but even more, he hadn't liked that anyone was so far down they'd live in a place like that. The woman needed mental help as well as a bulldozer to clean the place.

He handed her his cell phone. "Text George Ingram the following: Need 6, 22:00, Leather & Chains, dress code advised." His lips twitched, knowing what George's reaction would be.

Two seconds after Sachie hit send, his phone vibrated.

"You can answer," Teller said. "Put it on speaker."

"Yo, Osgood."

"Ingram," Teller acknowledged.

"Could you be more cryptic?" His friend and teammate always got straight to the point.

Teller chuckled. "My client and I need backup tonight at a motorcycle club."

"A single operative kind of backup or a potential team convergence bailout?"

"Hard to say. I'd lean toward team convergence. The guy we're going in to question is a recent prison release. My client helped convict him of child abuse.

He's also not averse to beating women, as his first stop post-prison was at his ex-girlfriend's place. He put her in the hospital. We assume his MC associates are equally pleasant."

"Gotcha," George said. "And by dress code, I assume you want us to blend in."

"We'd like to at least make it through the door," Teller said.

"I assume the client you're taking is Ms. Moore."

"News travels fast," Teller observed.

"Hawk gave us the heads-up in case you needed support," George explained. "You sure you want to take Ms. Moore into the middle of what sounds like a dangerous motorcycle gang? Is this something we can do without exposing her to the risk?"

"I'm going," Sachie said, with a stubborn set to her chin. "With or without the Brotherhood Protectors."

As Teller had predicted. That's part of the reason I wanted to get some additional insurance. We think the guy we're going after might be the one who has been at the root of her problems."

"Why not let the police handle it?" George asked.

Teller cocked an eyebrow in Sachie's direction.

"I've worked with the Honolulu and Hawaii police in the past. Sometimes, word leaks out to the wrong people," Sachie said. "I don't want anyone warning Finkel before I get some answers from him. Since we're not going to the bar until late tonight, I have some other places and people I want to check. It might change our direction."

"We just want the team ready if we have to go to Leather & Chains tonight," Teller added.

"On it," George said. "I'll rally the troops and wait on standby for the go-ahead."

"Roger," Teller said. "Out here."

"Out here," George echoed and ended the call.

"Where are we going next?" he asked.

Sachie's brow furrowed. "I'm thinking."

Before she could come to a conclusion, her cell phone rang. She frowned down at the display. "It's Dr. Janek," she said and answered. "Yes, sir."

The lines across her forehead eased. "Yes, sir. We'll stop by in a few minutes." After she ended the call, she gave Teller a brief smile. "Dr. Janek forgot to give me a stack of mail. I'd like to swing by and collect it. I'm not sure where to go next to find my stalker until we corner Travis at the club tonight, so I'd like to get in touch with Kylie, Luke's girlfriend."

She scrolled through the contacts on her cell phone, found what she was looking for and placed a call, putting the phone on speaker. "I hope Luke's foster family has Kylie's information."

The call rang three times before a woman's voice answered. "Ms. Moore?"

"Yes, Mrs. Randall, how are you and your husband?"

The woman sighed. "Okay, now that the reporters have stopped coming around. How are you?"

"Finally coming out of the fog and looking for answers."

"How can I help?" Mrs. Randall asked.

"I'd like to talk with Kylie, Luke's girlfriend. I know they had an argument, and that Kylie fell and got hurt. He blamed himself. I'm trying to piece together what made Luke feel like he had no other choice."

"He was head over heels for that girl," Mrs. Randall said. "I can't imagine him purposely hurting her."

"I agree. I'd like to hear Kylie's side of that argument," Sachie said. "Do you have her phone number?"

"Actually, I do. Thankfully, I got it from Luke when he started dating her, in case I couldn't get in touch with him on his own phone. Hold on, let me scroll through my contacts." The woman stopped talking for a few seconds and then came back with, "There she is. I'll share the contact."

A moment later, Sachie's cell phone beeped with an incoming text.

"I'm glad I had her number," Mrs. Randall said. "The police confiscated Luke's cell phone and have yet to return it. I hope you find out what was bothering Luke. My husband and I tried talking to him the last couple of weeks before he did what he did. We could tell all was not well in his world, but he wouldn't open up. He kept saying he was fine. At one point, I asked if I could help him with whatever problem he was having. I remember him saying, *I can handle it*." She paused. "I only wish I'd tried harder to get him to open up. I keep thinking he'd still be here if I'd been more persistent." She gave a brief laugh. "At the time, I thought there was a fine line between being persistent and pushy with teens. I didn't want to drive him away. I should've been pushy."

"We can't second-guess what happened," Sachie said. "It doesn't change the outcome. But we can learn. That's why I want to understand everything that led up to Luke's final decision."

"I'd like to know that as well," Mrs. Randall said. "If my husband and I decide to foster a teen again, which I doubt we will, I'd like to know how to get in front of the issue before it goes too far."

"Thank you for taking Luke in. I'm almost certain that whatever happened to send him over the edge had nothing to do with you and your husband. He only ever had good things to say about you."

"Thank you for that," Mrs. Randall said. "And if there's anything else I can do, don't hesitate to call."

Sachie ended the call and placed the next. It only rang once before voicemail picked up. "Hi, this is Kylie. I can't come to the phone right now. Leave a message, and I might return your call, that is, *if* you're not a telemarketer or a creepy stalker."

Sachie shot a smile toward Teller.

He liked it when she smiled. She'd had so little to smile about lately. He wanted to find her stalker and put an end to the terror he'd inspired. Then Sachie would have the time to heal and learn to smile more often.

"Kylie, this is Sachie Moore. I was Luke's counselor and was with him when he... passed." Sachie paused as if gathering her thoughts or courage. "I'd like to talk with you, if you're up to it. I'm trying to better understand what happened. No pressure. If you're not ready, I'll understand." She ended the call and sighed. "I hate opening the wounds. If she was half as crazy about him as he was about her, she's got to be a dark place right now. The shock of losing a friend so suddenly and violently can sometimes have a domino effect. I hope she's not dominoing."

Teller reached for her hand and held it for the rest of the drive to Dr. Janek's office.

The doctor was seated behind the receptionist's desk, looking at the computer monitor, his forehead creased in a deep frown. He glanced up at Sachie. "I can't make heads or tails of this appointment calendar."

Sachie slipped behind the desk and leaned over the doctor. "Let me."

He removed his hand from the mouse, and Sachie took control. "What were you trying to do?"

"I just spoke with a patient and needed to schedule his next appointment." He sat back far enough to let Sachie in to navigate the system. He gave her the date and time. "I checked against my schedule, and it will work. I just couldn't add it myself. Lindsey can't call in sick ever again."

"It's not as hard as you think," Sachie said. "Watch." She slowly led him through the steps to add an appointment to the calendar and backed out all the changes before committing them.

"Whoa, wait," he said, his eyebrows rising up his forehead. "Why did you remove the appointment?"

"You won't learn if you don't do it yourself," she said. "Now, you do it."

Teller had to choke back laughter at the doctor's incredulous expression.

But the man fiddled with the mouse and the keyboard until he sat back and nodded. "I did it."

"I always knew you could," Sachie said.

"I still don't want to be without a receptionist," he mumbled, then pushed back from the desk and stood. "What can I help you with?"

"You said you had a stack of mail for me," Sachie reminded him.

"Yes, yes. So I do." He turned to a credenza behind him, grabbed a stack of envelopes and handed them to Sachie.

"Some of it's junk mail, but I'll let you decide. "Have you had any luck chasing down your trouble-maker?" he asked.

"Not so far," Sachie said.

"Let me know if you need anything else. I'll be here another hour before I call it a day." He walked into his office, calling out over his shoulder, "In the meantime, I need to make notes and prepare for my next patient."

"Thank you, Dr. Janek." Sachie gathered her mail and left the building.

Teller opened the car door and waited for her to slide into her seat. Then he closed the door and got in the other side. "We still have all day before we have to be at the bar. Are there any other patients who might be angry with you?"

Sachie shook her head. "My patients are usually happy to see me. It's the family members of the children I recommend to be removed from their homes who have the biggest beef with me. Luke was an anomaly—a tragic one at that. I feel compelled to discover his reason for feeling like he had to die to find peace, and compelled isn't the right word. I've moved on to obsessed."

"Like you, Mrs. Randall felt a strong sense of responsibility for what happened with Luke," Teller offered.

"Guilt is a huge emotional factor for me. I should've done more."

"You couldn't have guessed what he was about to do. Just like Mrs. Randall. How many of her foster kids have committed suicide?"

"None, until Luke," Sachie said.

"And how many of your patients have committed suicide?" Teller asked.

"Luke was my first." She closed her eyes and squeezed her hands together. "Please let him be the last."

As he sat with his hands on the steering wheel and no direction to go, Teller nodded toward the stack of mail in Sachie's lap. "You want to go through those letters while we stew on where we'll go next?"

"I almost forgot." Sachie sat up straight and flipped through the junk mail, tossing some envelopes onto the dash, unopened. The sender of the next letter had handwritten the street, city, state and zip code, and addressed the envelope to "Miss Sachie."

A faint smile lifted the corners of Sachie's lips as she carefully opened the envelope. Inside was a card that appeared to have been drawn by a child using colorful crayons.

A big heart graced the front of the card, colored in with red.

Sachie opened the card. *THANK YOU* was spelled out with large capital letters in blue crayon. The author and artist had added *for being my friend* and then signed it *Emma*.

"A fan of yours?" Teller asked.

"Apparently." Sachie stared at the card, her eyes shining with unshed tears. "Emma was having nightmares when her mother brought her to see me. In fact, her mother and father weren't doing much better. Emma's little brother had gotten off the bus before Emma. He ran across the street without looking first. A car hit him. Emma witnessed it."

"Did the boy survive?"

Sachie shook her head. "They went from being a cute little family of four to a family of three heartbroken people. I saw Emma for several months, helping her work through her feelings."

"She felt responsible, didn't she?" Teller guessed.

Sachie nodded. "She was the older sister and should've been holding his hand. However, Dalton was a force to be reckoned with—headstrong and in constant motion. If the driver hadn't been looking down at his cell phone, he would've seen the bus had stopped and the lights were blinking red. Vehicles are supposed to stop when school buses are loading and unloading."

"Poor Emma," Teller commented. "That's a horrible thing for a child to witness."

Sachie nodded. "I'm glad she's doing much better." Her lips pressed together. "And yes, I see the parallels to what happened with me and Luke. I know it takes time to get past the horror."

She flipped through more junk mail, laying the letters with the others on the dash, and then stopped to read a glossy postcard depicting boys playing in a gym. "This is the Boys' Club where Luke worked after school. They're having an open house..." she turned the card over, "today, actually." Her forehead wrinkled as she tapped the card to her chin. "When I was asking Luke what was wrong, he wouldn't tell me. I asked him if something had happened at school. He said no. Then I asked him if something had happened at the Boys' Club."

"Did he say yes?"

Sachie shook her head. "No. But he didn't say no. He avoided answering the question."

"I say we go to the Boys' Club next." Teller entered the address in his map application on his cell phone. As he pulled out onto the road, Sachie's cell phone rang.

She answered with, "This is Sachie. Kylie?" She glanced toward Teller. "Hold on." She lowered the phone and placed it in speaker mode. "Are you okay?"

"Yes, ma'am. I'm sorry I couldn't answer your earlier call. I've had so many crank calls that my mother doesn't want me answering any. She turned off my phone. I just happened to turn it back on to see someone had left a message."

"Thank you for returning my call," Sachie said.

"You were the counselor Luke was seeing?"

"Yes," Sachie said.

"Wow," the one word sounded choked with emotion. "You were there... You saw..." An audible sniff sounded over the line.

"Yes. Probably like you, I've been struggling to process it all."

"Struggling," Kylie said, the word breaking on what sounded like a sob. "Yeah."

"Before he..." Sachie stopped.

Teller glanced toward her.

Her eyes were filled with tears.

Teller found an empty parking lot and pulled in. He reached for Sachie's hand and held it.

She gave him a weak smile, swallowed and continued. "Luke asked me to tell you he was sorry for dragging you into his shitty life, and that he was sorry he hurt you."

"Oh, God," Kylie whispered. "He said that?"

"Yes. I'm so sorry I didn't deliver the message sooner," Sachie said softly, tears slipping down her cheeks.

Teller gently squeezed Sachie's hand, wishing he could take away her pain, knowing he couldn't.

"Now that I can think more clearly," Sachie said, "I'm trying to understand what drove Luke to that...day."

"It's all my fault," Kylie said. "We had a terrible argument."

"What was the argument about, Kylie?" Sachie asked.

"He was so angry," Kylie's voice caught in a sob, "it scared me."

"Angry with you?" Sachie persisted, her voice calm, controlled and so gentle that Teller would have told her anything she wanted to know just to keep her talking.

"Not at me. At something that happened where he worked. He said they were pushing him to do something he didn't want to do."

"Did he tell you what that was?"

"No. He wouldn't say, no matter how many times I asked. I asked him if it was illegal. He wouldn't say. I asked him if it would hurt the kids. He said not at the club, but that if he didn't do it, they would hurt his best friend."

"Did he say who *they* were?"

"No. He wouldn't tell me anything. That's what made me mad." She paused. "The last time he saw me, I was mad. And I wasn't even mad at him. I was mad at whoever was pushing him to do whatever it was he didn't feel right doing. But I took it out on Luke. I didn't get to tell him I loved him." Her voice faded off.

Teller bit down on his tongue to keep from firing off all the questions that crowded his mind. Kylie didn't know another person was listening in. He couldn't be certain how she'd react if she did. And Sachie was the professional counselor and doing a good job of wading through the heartbroken teenage girl's emotions to get to the facts.

"Kylie, what friend was he worried about?" Sachie asked in that same, soft, caring tone.

"Mark," Kylie said. "When Luke started working

at the club, Mark showed him around. He learned that Mark had come from a broken home and didn't like his stepfather. They bonded over their poor excuses for fathers and video games. They even traded some of those games."

Teller wanted the girl to get back to her argument with Luke. Patience wasn't always his strong suit.

It was Sachie's. His respect for the counselor grew stronger by the minute. What made him fall for her even more was how much she cared for her patients and how far she'd go to figure out where she'd gone wrong with the one she'd failed.

"Was Luke very close to Mark?" Sachie prompted.

"Sometimes, too close. Luke said they thought so much alike, it was as if they shared thoughts. He said they finished each other's sentences." Kylie snorted softly. "At first, I was a little jealous, but Luke still made time for me, and he'd never really had a good guy friend. He said Mark was like the brother he'd never had."

"There were other children in his foster home," Sachie pointed out.

"Not like Mark."

"Did you meet Mark?" Sachie asked. "What was he like?"

"Luke wanted me to meet him, but the timing wasn't right. They went their separate ways once they left the club. Luke would come spend time with me, and Mark went to his home. Then Luke started changing. He went from being happy and doing well in school to frowning all the time. Where we used to talk nonstop on the phone well into the night, our calls got shorter and shorter. He wouldn't tell me what was wrong. I thought he wanted to break up with me. When I told him that, he got angry. He said he loved me, but he had a lot on his mind. I pushed and pushed until he blew up and said all those things about someone threatening to hurt his best friend if he didn't do whatever it was they wanted."

"Did Luke say how they would hurt Mark if he didn't do what they wanted?"

"No. Just that he couldn't let it happen, even if it meant doing what they wanted." Kylie huffed. "Whatever it was must've been bad for Luke to be so upset about it."

"Luke said he couldn't let you do something. That he grabbed your arm to stop you, and that's when you fell," Sachie said.

"I told him to go to the police and turn them in. He said he couldn't. It would make things worse. He didn't say how. So, I told him I was going to go to the Boys' Club and find whoever it was trying to get Luke to do something he didn't want to do and tell them to back off." She gave a shaky laugh. "I didn't know how I would do that, considering Luke didn't tell me anything useful. I just couldn't stand by and watch the guy I loved drifting further and further away. He grabbed my arm. I yanked it free. The next thing I remember was waking up in the hospital with a headache, only to learn my boyfriend had committed suicide."

"Oh, Kylie. I'm so sorry."

"You were there," Kylie said. "What happened?"

"He told me basically what you just said, and he blamed himself for hurting you. He didn't want to be like his father and was afraid that he was."

"He was nothing like his father," Kylie said. "Nothing. He was kind and caring, and I loved him for who he was.

"He really loved you, too," Sachie said. "He thought the only way to protect the ones he loved was to do what he did."

"He was wrong," Kylie cried. "I died when he died."

Sachie didn't respond to the girl's comment. Nothing would make her feel better at that moment.

Teller knew how hard it was to lose someone you loved, but he also knew that the living kept living. Kylie was young. The heartache would fade over time.

"Kylie, if you ever need to talk to someone, you have my phone number now. Please, call me."

"Thank you," Kylie said. "I feel like you might be the only one who really understands."

"I feel the same about you," Sachie said.

"I have to go before my mother comes looking for me," Kylie said. "She hovers over me like I might break at any moment and even has me homeschooling. I haven't left the house in two weeks. I think she's got me on suicide watch."

Teller's heart squeezed hard in his chest. If Kylie were his daughter, he'd have done the same.

"Ms. Moore, Luke was a good guy. He had a big heart and only wanted to be loved. Promise you'll let me know if you find out who was tearing him apart," Kylie said. "I'd really like to see them rot in hell."

When Sachie ended the call, she stared at their joined hands for a long moment, her face pale, her mouth set in a grim line. When she looked up, Teller saw fierce determination burning in her eyes. "They're having an open house at the Boys' Club. I think we need to check it out."

Teller briefly squeezed her hand again and then drove out of the parking lot.

Paying a visit to the Boys' Club might not get them any closer to the person stalking her, but Teller wouldn't hold Sachie back from learning the truth about the young man who'd taken his own life in front of her.

# CHAPTER 14

AFTER HER CONVERSATION WITH KYLIE, Sachie sat silently, unmoving and emotionally drained. Hearing the heartache in the teen's tone and her anguished feeling that she hadn't done enough to save Luke, mirrored everything Sachie felt.

Whether she was on a quest to seek justice for Luke or to redeem herself for failing him, she had to know what had driven him to take his own life. The Boys' Club, or someone near it, had held a threat over Luke's head, one he ultimately couldn't live with.

Sachie was fired up and ready to go into battle for her dead patient. Not that it would bring him back, but maybe by finding the assholes who'd pushed him to the edge, she could stop them from doing the same to another susceptible teen.

And while she was at the club, she'd look for

Luke's friend Mark and make sure he wasn't in the same predicament Luke had found himself in.

As Teller pulled into the parking lot, Sachie glanced his way, her heart swelling. She couldn't have come this far without the support of the former Delta Force protector. Her hand remained warm from when he'd held it throughout her conversation with Kylie. He was there to protect her, not to hold her hand or hold her through the night when she had nightmares.

She wouldn't be as confident going into the Boys' Club by herself. She'd do it to find out what had spooked Luke into ending his life. Having Teller with her made her more confident.

"The building looks to be in good repair," Teller noted. "I'm not excited about the buildings surrounding it. The neighborhood seems a little sketchy to me."

Sachie agreed with his initial assessment. "I noticed some graffiti on some of the buildings. There are probably some gangs in the area."

"Hopefully, the club keeps some kids off the streets and out of gangs." He turned to Sachie. "So what's it going to be? Are we going in guns blazing, demanding answers?"

Sachie shook her head. "We don't know if it was people inside the facility putting the pressure on Luke or someone in the area around it."

"Then we should probably go in, look around and

ask what the Boys' Club is doing for the at-risk kids in this area," Teller offered. "It's a legitimate concern for a counselor working with troubled teens."

"Right. That covers me. I am a counselor." She raised an eyebrow. "What about you?"

"I'm your fiancé, along for the ride. We're going to dinner after we tour the facility."

Sachie's pulse quickened at Teller's words. Her fiancé? She'd never considered marriage. Never really thought she could trust a man with her physical well-being, much less her heart.

Having spent less than two days with Teller, she truly believed he would never willingly hurt her and that she could trust him with her life.

As for her heart...

It wasn't a matter of trusting him not to break it. It was more a question of whether he would even want her heart. She preached the importance of believing in yourself and marched to that chorus. She believed in herself as an individual, strong enough to survive on her own. She didn't need anyone to make her happy. That was all on her. But did she really believe a good man could love her after all she'd endured? That he could get past the incest inflicted on her body and soul to love the woman who'd come out of that chapter of her life heavily scarred, but stronger?

"Does that work for you?" Teller asked as he killed the engine and released his seatbelt buckle.

Sachie blinked to pull herself back to reality. "Yes. That works." She pushed open her door and started to get out but couldn't. She must have been more flustered by the idea of being Teller's fiancée than she'd thought. She'd forgotten to unbuckle her own seatbelt.

Heat rising up her neck into her cheeks, she released the buckle and jumped out, hoping Teller hadn't seen her struggle or guessed that she was affected by his announcement.

They entered the large building that housed a gymnasium down the middle and a number of smaller rooms lining either side. A man in a royal blue T-shirt stood with his back to the entrance, watching young boys playing basketball in the gymnasium. When he turned and realized Teller and Sachie had entered, a smile stretched across his face. "Welcome to the Honolulu Boys' Club. Have you come for the open house?" he asked.

Sachie nodded. "We have."

"Great." The man held out his hand to Sachie. "I'm Grant Simmons, the director."

"Sachie Moore." Sachie shook the man's hand and turned to the man beside her. "This is my...fiancé, Teller Osgood." A little thrill shivered through her. Calling Teller her fiancé felt weird and strangely right at the same time. Maybe she was finally getting past her marriage phobia. Whatever it was, she didn't need to be thinking about marriage, especially with a man who'd been hired to protect her.

"Well, tell me, Ms. Moore, are you and your fiancé looking to the future at what options are available in this area for after-school programs? Or would you like us to add you to the waitlist for immediate placement if an opening becomes available?"

Heat burned Sachie's cheeks again.

Kids? She hadn't even considered kids because she hadn't dreamed of ever marrying until an extremely sexy, hunk of a Delta Force guy suggested they pretend to be engaged.

Now, she was falling down a rabbit hole of unrealistic possibilities.

"No. Not yet, anyway," Teller answered for her, placing a hand at the small of her back. "My beautiful fiancée is a counselor for troubled teens and children from less-than-ideal home situations. She wanted to check out what the Boys' Club could offer some of her kids."

"Perfect," Simmons said. "We have a full-time staff of myself, an administrative assistant and a janitor. We employ older students as leaders in the after-school program, who keep the boys moving and learning. We also have volunteers who fill in when they're needed and available. Although we're down two after-school leaders, we're actively recruiting to fill those positions."

"Do you have high turnover of your teen leaders?" Sachie asked.

"Not often," the director said. "Although they eventually age out and move on to college or the workforce."

Sachie knew why they were down at least one of their leaders. The director was smart not to mention they'd lost one to suicide. It could be bad for business.

Simmons led them down a hallway flanked by rooms with tables and chairs, explaining the kids had study time to work on their homework as well as activities to expand their minds through art and music.

"We want the boys to have a rich environment of learning and moving to keep them physically and mentally healthy. Our gymnasium allows them to learn skills in different sports and learn the value of teamwork."

They stepped into the gym where a couple dozen boys of different ages and sizes drilled in different skills involving basketballs.

At one end of the gym, a teenage boy worked with the smaller kids, demonstrating how to bounce a basketball, alternating hands.

At the other end of the gym, preteens and teens were engaged in a half-court game, each team wearing different-colored bibs. In the middle of the teens was an adult who stood taller than most of the kids around him.

Sachie's eyes narrowed. The man looked familiar, but he was moving quickly and was a little too far away for her to see clearly.

"Speaking of volunteers," Director Simmons nodded toward the adult at the far end of the gym. "That's one of our frequent volunteers. His full-time job is as a police officer with the Hawaii Police Department. He's a regular, showing up for an hour or two a couple of times a week. The older kids like it when he plays basketball with them, as you can see."

"Is that Officer Roland?" Sachie asked.

"Yes, ma'am, it is," the director grinned. "Do you know him?"

She nodded, glad she'd figured out who it was. Knowing there was an off-duty police officer in the building made her feel they might want to concentrate their search for bad guys in the buildings surrounding the club.

Roland stepped away from the kids, leaving them to continue playing without him. He crossed the gym floor in his shorts and sweaty T-shirt, coming to a stop in front of Sachie and Teller. "Ms. Moore, I didn't expect to see you here. What brings you around?"

"I'm always looking for places parents can count on to keep their children occupied with other alternatives to cell phones and video games."

"What do you think so far?" Roland waved a hand toward the gym and the kids actively engaged.

Sachie nodded. "Mr. Simmons has taken us on the grand tour. I like that the club provides a much-needed service to the youth of the city who might otherwise not have the resources to afford what it offers."

Roland gave a brief nod. "The staff is committed to giving the kids a safe environment to be kids."

The director's cell phone buzzed. He glanced at the display. "I've been expecting this call. I need to take it. Please excuse me. Officer Roland can answer any questions you may have." The director walked away as he answered his phone.

Roland lowered his voice. "I heard you've had some issues with a stalker? Have you had any luck identifying who it is?"

Sachie shook her head. "Not yet."

The officer frowned. "You don't think he's here, do you?"

"No," Sachie said. "I'm trying to get some closure on a teen who used to work here."

"The one who committed suicide?" Roland shook his head. "Tragic loss. Luke was a good kid. He had a bright future ahead of him."

"Did you have much interaction with him?" Sachie asked.

"Not too often," Roland said. "We occasionally played basketball with the kids."

Sachie glanced around, her gaze landing on the teen leader working with the smaller kids.

"During my sessions with Luke, he talked about another teen he worked with here—a kid named Mark. Is he here today?"

"He was. I think he left a few minutes ago. You probably just missed him. What did you want with Mark?"

"Does he have a last name?" Teller asked.

The officer nodded. "Bradford."

"I understand they were good friends," Sachie said. "I wanted to talk to him about Luke's behavior leading up to his death. I hope to gain some insight into why he felt compelled to end his life." Sachie's gaze went to the teens still playing basketball behind Roland. "I want to know what made him so desperate that he felt he didn't have another option."

"Did he mention any troubles he might have had at school?" Roland asked.

"No. Did he have any issues with anyone here at the Boys' Club?" Sachie asked.

"I didn't notice any, but then I wasn't here all the time."

Sachie sighed. "I guess I'll have to come back when Mark's here. Maybe Luke opened up with him."

"Mark's usually here every weekday." Roland glanced across the gym. "You might catch him tomorrow. I'd better get back to the boys. I hope you find what you're looking for."

"Thank you."

"Can you find your way out?" Roland asked.

"Yes, sir."

Roland hurried back to the game.

Sachie's gaze swept through the gym. "Who else can we ask about Luke?"

"Not the kids," Teller said.

"Definitely not the kids," Sachie said. "Should we try to track down Mark at his home?"

"Now that we have a last name, I can get Swede to work his magic. He should be able to find his address." Teller texted the name to Swede. "Are you ready to go?"

Sachie looked one last time, trying to imagine Luke on the gym floor working with the little kids, teaching them how to shoot hoops that were so far above them it was comical to watch their attempts.

She sighed. "I'm ready."

As they walked to the exit, Sachie saw a tall, lanky young man with thick black hair exiting the building. Something about him made her look twice. At that exact moment, he glanced over his shoulder.

Sachie's heart stopped for a full second and then slammed into her ribs. "Luke?" she whispered. Turning to Teller, she asked, "Did you see that young man?"

Teller had glanced over his shoulder back toward the gym. When he focused ahead of where they stood, he frowned. "See what?"

"The teen who just stepped out of the complex. I swear... I mean the resemblance..." She scrubbed a hand down her face and rubbed her eyes. "I must be hallucinating again. He looked just like Luke."

Teller hurried with her out the front entrance. Sachie stopped, looked in both directions and saw...nothing.

Teller cupped her elbow and walked toward their parked sedan. They were halfway across the parking lot when a flurry of movement whipped past Sachie. Her purse was ripped off her shoulder before she could wrap her fingers around the strap.

"Hey!" she yelled automatically.

"Son of a bitch," Teller muttered and took off after the thief. "Sachie, get into the car and lock the doors," he called out over his shoulder.

For a solid five seconds, Sachie stood frozen to the spot. Then she moved, heading toward the sedan. She'd rather have gone after the assailant, but she knew she'd only slow Teller's pursuit. And if she didn't get into the sedan and lock the doors, Teller might turn back and make sure she did, losing the thief in the process.

When she reached the sedan, she climbed in, locked the doors and waited for what felt like a very long time, hoping Teller wouldn't get hurt. She'd rather lose everything in her purse than have Teller harmed in the process of trying to retrieve it.

After a while, Sachie got anxious and worried that

Teller wasn't back yet. She unlocked the sedan and stepped out into the afternoon sunshine.

Her pulse quickened at the sight of big, broad-shouldered Teller. With one hand securing a man's arm behind his back, Teller shoved the man forward until he was close enough for Sachie to see that he wasn't Luke or Luke's lookalike.

The man had fully tattooed sleeves on both arms. The sleeves extended down to the back of the man's hands, where a small pyramid with an eye in the middle of it stared at Sachie. The guy wore baggy clothing, his hair was unkempt and he appeared to be high on something.

"Sachie, could you call 911 and have them come prepared to process a thief?" Teller said.

Before she could dial, Officer Roland stepped out of the building wearing jeans, a T-shirt and running shoes. "What's going on?" he asked.

"This man stole Ms. Moore's purse," Teller said. "We were just about to contact 911 so they could send a police officer to take him in."

Roland shook his head. "I'll make that call and take care of him. Sachie, I have your number. We can get your statement later. I'm sure you two have other things to do."

"We don't mind staying until the police arrive," Sachie assured Roland.

"Not to worry. I have this. I'll take him into the office and hold him until the cops on duty arrive.

Take care. I'll see you two again soon." He took control of holding the man's arm between his shoulder blades and marched him into the facility.

Teller handed Sachie her purse. "Check to make sure he didn't take anything. I don't think he had time but check anyway."

She glanced at the contents in her purse and pulled out her wallet to count the credit cards. "Everything's here."

"Well, since your Officer Roland is going to take him in, we can head out," Teller said.

"We still have eight or nine hours to burn before we head to the Leather & Chains," Sachie said. "Is it possible to find a thrift shop for biker babe clothing and then a hotel? I'm exhausted, and I'm not the one who was in a fight to reclaim my purse."

"We can do both those things. I could stand to rest for a couple of hours before we head into a biker bar." He held the door for Sachie.

"I'm sure it won't be as easy as touring the Boys' Club." She slipped into the passenger seat and settled her purse on her lap.

Teller slid into the driver's seat, frowning. "I'd feel better if you didn't go."

Sachie stiffened. She understood his concern, but he needed her. "I know what Travis looks like," she said. "You and your friends don't."

Teller sighed and started the engine. "You have a

point," he said and shifted into reverse. "You know how to make my job difficult."

"You don't have to come," she said, hoping he didn't decide to back out.

He snorted. "You're not getting rid of me that easily."

Her heart lightened at his teasing and at the relief she felt that he would be at her side as they stepped into a bar filled with a potentially dangerous gang of bikers. She hoped Teller and his team wouldn't be hurt in her pursuit of her stalker. Maybe they'd blend right in, observe Travis, get him alone and then what?

Force him to confess to terrorizing her?

How well would that go over surrounded by his gang of cut-throat bikers?

Sachie wasn't feeling all that confident about this plan. Hopefully, they'd come up with a better alternative in the seven hours they had before they showed up at Leather & Chains.

# CHAPTER 15

A QUICK TRIP to a secondhand store netted the majority of the clothing they needed to blend in at the Leather & Chains biker bar. A side trip to a motorcycle accessories shop helped them find the items they hoped would complete their disguises without spending a lot of money.

"We still have at least six hours to kill before we converge on our target," Teller said. "What do you want to do?"

"I've been so tense today, I'm tired and my muscles are knotted." Sachie rolled her shoulders. "What I'd really like to do is to take a hot shower and lie down for a while. Sleep would be even better, but that's not going to happen with a mission looming." She shook her head. "How did you Special Ops guys do it? It had to be insanely nerve-wracking, prepping for a mission and then waiting for the event."

Teller's lips twisted at the memories of missions where waiting had been key. "We learned to sleep whenever and wherever we were, not knowing how long we'd be out or when we'd get the chance to close our eyes."

"Hopefully, we won't be up all night looking for Travis," Sachie said. "I'm not even sure what we should do when, or if, we find him."

"I thought we were going to ask him if he's the one who's been stalking you," Teller said, knowing exactly how insane that sounded.

Sachie must have had the same thought. She glanced at him as if he'd grown a third ear. "Do you think he's going to calmly confess to it?" Her gaze went out the front windshield. "I want to find out who's at the bottom of it, but I don't want to get killed in the process. And I don't want you or the members of your team to suffer because of me. Maybe we should call it all off. Or we could do a stakeout, wait for Travis to show up and follow him to wherever he goes after the bar, get him alone and ask him then."

"You're getting yourself all worked up about something that isn't going to happen for another six hours." He reached across the console and took her hand. "We'll make it work one way or another. In the meantime, let's get you that hot shower. And if your muscles are still knotted, I could be convinced to massage out the knots."

She gave him a weak smile. "You'd do that?"

Teller read her response as positive and his pulse quickened. "Whatever it takes." He squeezed her hand briefly and returned his to the steering wheel. "You need to conserve energy. We don't know what's going to happen tonight. We'll need to be ready for anything."

He pulled into the drive-through, loading and unloading area of a high-rise hotel.

Sachie frowned at the elaborate entrance. "I don't know if I can afford this. Couldn't we go somewhere that won't break my bank?"

He chuckled. "I get a military discount here. Plus, they have a great restaurant and quick room service." He cut the engine. "Besides, it's just one night."

"If we get back here after we find Travis." She stared at the fancy hotel. "We could be spending a lot of money for a room we might not get to use all night."

"We get to use the room for the best part of the night, to include a hot shower, room service and a comfortable bed to relax on. We didn't get that kind of treatment before each mission in the Army. I consider it a perk of being a civilian." He winked and got out of the sedan. Then he rounded the hood and opened her door for her.

She got out slowly, glancing down at her jeans and casual blouse. "I'm not dressed for a place like this."

"You look amazing," he said, and meant it. She'd look good in anything she wore or in nothing at all. His groin tightened automatically at that last thought. He grabbed the bags with their purchases from the back seat and their suitcases from the trunk.

Clutching her purse in front of her, Sachie fell in step with Teller as the glass door slid open and a rush of chilled air washed over them.

After running down the purse thief, he was hot and sticky. When Sachie had mentioned wanting a hot shower, this hotel had been the first thing that had come to his mind.

Right after wicked images of Sachie standing naked in the hot shower with shiny rivulets of water cascading over her skin.

Yeah, he could keep dreaming. The woman had enough problems without having her hired body-guard coming on to her.

Though he couldn't wash that image out of his mind, he pushed it to the back of his thoughts and secured a room with two queen-sized beds. He didn't want her to think she'd have to share one with him.

Unless she wanted to. He wasn't opposed to the idea. Though, it would take all his willpower to keep from touching her the way he wanted to touch her—not just holding her in his arms through a nightmare or holding her hand.

The more his thoughts went down that path, the

more he believed being alone in a hotel room with Sachie was a bad idea. He almost handed the key card back to the clerk and walked Sachie back out to the sedan.

Instead, he gave her the keycard, collected their bags and walked with her to the elevator, playing it as cool as he could when his blood burned hot through his veins. Whatever he did, he couldn't let her know he was extremely attracted to her. He didn't want her to feel awkward about sharing a room with him, and he couldn't leave her in a room by herself.

They rode the elevator up to the fifth floor. Their room was near the end of the hallway, three doors down from the stairwell, Teller noted.

Sachie skimmed the keycard over the reader. The lock clicked open, and she pushed the door inward.

The room smelled of new carpet and fresh paint. Obviously, it had been redecorated recently. The furniture looked new, and the bed linens were crisp and bright.

Sachie went straight to the window. Although the hotel wasn't directly on the shore, like many on Waikiki Beach, it had a view of the ocean in the distance.

"You can have the shower first," Teller said. "I want to touch base with the team and with Hawk. I also want to see if Swede has come up with anything new."

"Sounds good." She remained at the window a moment longer, then sighed and lifted her suitcase onto the bed. After extracting a T-shirt, panties and a pair of shorts, she headed for the bathroom.

Teller called Hawk and filled him in on what had happened that day and their plan to go to the biker bar that evening.

"I've been in touch with George Ingram," Hawk said. "They'll come with four; plus you, it's five. Do I need to send some over from Maui?"

"God, I hope not," Teller said. "I'm considering doing a stakeout instead of going into the bar. It would be easier to corner Travis alone for questioning."

"And you won't have to put Sachie in danger by taking her into the bar," Hawk added.

"Exactly," Teller said. "George's four-man team can wait outside as well. If we need to go in, they'll be there."

"I like that better than storming a bar full of motorcycle club gang members. I ran the bar name by Swede. He's doing research now."

"Good. He's next on my list to call."

"Then I won't hold you up," Hawk said. "Make sure you work with George's team and gear up with comm equipment. You'll want to be able to communicate in case you need to split up."

"Roger," Teller said. "I'll let you know how it goes."

"Out here," Hawk said.

Teller ended that call and placed one to George, arranging a time and place to meet. George had communications equipment that would help them keep in touch without relying on their cell phones. The Brotherhood Protectors had an array of radio headsets, much like they'd used on special operations missions all over the world. When they met, they could discuss the plan and be ready for whatever scenario unfolded.

Before he could call Swede, the bathroom door opened, and Sachie emerged in a loud of steam, wearing a long, loose T-shirt that hung down to mid-thigh and with a towel wrapped turban-style around her hair. Barefoot and makeup-free, she was sexy as hell.

For a moment, all Teller could do was stare at her, noting her long, slender legs and the way her breasts made points against the fabric of the shirt.

When he brought his focus up to her eyes, she met his gaze and held it.

"The bathroom's all yours," she said softly.

Teller wanted to say something but couldn't think of anything other than how beautiful she was. Unsure of what her response might be, and not wanting to make things awkward, he bit down hard on his tongue, grabbed his bag and ducked into the bathroom.

He spent a solid ten minutes beneath a cool spray, hoping to bring his desire in check. By the time he'd dried off and dressed in a pair of shorts, he was able to walk out of the bathroom without an embarrassing tent in his shorts. He considered that a win.

Until he stepped into the room and found Sachie seated on one of the beds, one of her legs stretched out in front of her, the other bent. She'd pulled the turban off her head and had brushed her damp, long blond hair back from her forehead, exposing the fine bones of her cheeks and the length of her neck.

Yeah, he wasn't as in control of his desire as he'd thought. As his groin tightened, Teller turned away.

His cell phone chirped, indicating an incoming text. It gave Teller something else to think about other than his obsession with the woman on the bed. The text was from Swede. He'd been the next call he was going to make after he'd showered. He brought up the message, which was an image of a tattoo on a man's arm. The tattoo was a pyramid with an eye in the middle that was strangely familiar.

Teller's phone chirped with another incoming text from Swede. This one had a link.

An article appeared about a gang in Honolulu called the All-Seeing Gang, suspected of working with the Sinaloa cartel out of Mexico, trafficking drugs in Hawaii. Members were identified by tattoos of a pyramid with an eye in the middle. Teller scrolled down the article, and another image of a pyramid tattoo appeared with an eye in the middle.

"That's the same tattoo as the guy who stole my

purse today." Sachie had come to stand beside Teller and peered over his arm at the article on his cell phone. She looked up into Teller's eyes. "That gang member was right there in front of the Boys' Club. Do you think they're pressuring kids to help them push drugs?"

"Could be," Teller said.

"When Luke was in my office that day, he talked about trading one drug for another and not wishing addiction on anyone. Luke had been court-ordered to see me after being caught with cocaine. He'd gone through rehab and had been clean for a while. But he needed help with mood swings. He was diagnosed with bipolar disorder and was prescribed medication to help him control the swings."

Sachie paced the length of the room and back, her head down, her brow furrowed. "He'd gone off the medication. He said something about trading one drug for another and that he never wanted to get back into drugs and didn't want anything to do with any drugs. I thought it was all about his medications. But if someone was trying to get him to distribute drugs by threatening to hurt his best friend, I could see why he was so distraught." She looked up, her gaze meeting Teller's. "He didn't want to deal drugs, but he didn't want them to hurt his best friend. They'd have no reason to hurt his friend if he wasn't around to intimidate." She shook her head, tears welling in her eyes.

Teller couldn't stand to see her so sad. He closed the distance between them and pulled her into his arms. "Why didn't he go to the police?"

As he pulled her close, Sachie's hands rested on his chest. "He said he couldn't go to the police."

"Did he say why? Were they threatening harm to his friend if he told anyone?"

She shook her head. "He didn't say."

"I'm surprised he didn't go to your cop friend, Roland." Teller held her for several minutes and even pressed a soft kiss to the top of her hair. "Hopefully, we'll learn more when we go to the Leather & Chains bar." However, the more he thought about it, the less he wanted to take Sachie. Drug cartels and people who dealt with them were ruthless.

Teller's cell phone rang, forcing him to give up his hold on Sachie.

She stepped back as he answered the call.

When he saw it was Swede, he put him on speaker. "Swede, you have me and Sachie on speaker."

"Good. I did some digging into the DEA's work following the Sinaloa cartel's infiltration into Hawaii. The cartel has connections with the All-Seeing gang. There've been several murders linked to the gang recently. They like to hang out at biker bars on the outskirts of Honolulu, one in particular."

Teller's gut clenched. "Leather & Chains?"

"That's the one."

"We ran into one of their members outside the

Boys' Club where Sachie's suicide victim worked. He had the pyramid with the eye tattoo."

"Whatever you do, be careful. Hawk said you have some of the team as backup."

"Yes, we do."

"I hope it's enough," Swede said. "Oh, and another interesting thing I found… I was looking into Sachie's Luke Stevenson. His father murdered his mother and is serving time in prison."

"We know," Sachie said. "He was worried he would have his father's genetic predisposition for violence. It was one of the reasons he killed himself."

"Wow," Swede said softly. "Then he didn't know."

Sachie glanced up at Teller, her brow furrowing. "Know what?"

"The man in jail wasn't his biological father," Swede paused. "He was adopted as an infant."

Sachie covered her mouth, tears welling in her eyes. "He didn't know."

"I found his birth record," Swede continued. "He was one of two live births. Luke was a twin."

Sachie leaned into Teller.

He circled her waist with his free hand and pulled her close. "Do you have any information about the other twin?"

"Not yet," Swede said. "It was a closed adoption. I'm working on it."

"Were they born in Hawaii?" Teller asked.

"Yes. And Luke's adoption was there in Hawaii."

"Anything else?" Teller asked.

"No, sir," Swede said. "I'll let you know if I learn anything else."

"Thanks," Teller said.

"If you're still bent on checking out the bar where the All-Seeing Gang hangs out, be careful. They play for keeps."

Teller understood the danger. "Roger." After he ended the call, he laid his cell phone on the dresser behind him and hugged Sachie closer.

"He was so afraid he'd be like his father," Sachie said. "He blamed himself for hurting Kylie and attributed it to his father's genes."

"And the father he knew wasn't his father at all," Teller concluded.

"Between the threat to his best friend and his own perceived threat to his girlfriend, Luke didn't see any other way out." Sachie pressed her forehead to his chest. "It didn't have to be that way."

Teller tipped her chin up and stared down into her eyes. "I'm so sorry for what happened to Luke." He kissed her forehead. "I'm sorry you had to witness it." He cupped the back of her neck and pressed his lips against her right temple. "If I could undo it all, I would."

She stared up into his eyes. "You can't."

"No." He touched his lips to her left temple.

"But you can hold me," she whispered.

A slight smile pulled his lips upward. "Yes, but only if you want me to."

She nodded. "I do. Please."

Teller chuckled and pressed his cheek against her hair. "Sweetheart, I already am."

"No," she whispered. "Closer."

He leaned back, his brow furrowing. "Closer?"

She nodded, her gaze holding his. "Only if you want to."

"Oh, I want to," he said. "More than I've ever wanted to hold a woman in my life. But help me out here. You're amazing and beautiful, with a huge heart that cares about so many. I don't want to hurt you in any way whatsoever. So, help me out here. I'll need a little more information." He stared into her eyes, trying to read her thoughts and failing miserably. "Just how close?"

A crooked smile curled her pretty pink lips. Sachie took his hand and stepped backward. "To be perfectly clear... I want you to hold me close enough..." she took another step backward, drawing him with her, "...close enough our skin will touch." Another step brought them closer to one of the beds. "Close enough, I can feel your heart beating against mine." Another step, and the backs of her legs rested against the end of the mattress. "Close enough to make love to me."

Teller's pulse raced through his body, pushing molten hot blood south to his groin. Still, he had to

ELLE JAMES

be sure. "Don't get me wrong. I want nothing more than to strip you naked and explore every inch of your body, making love to you."

Her brow dipped. "Here comes the but."

He nodded. "But you've been through so much, are you sure this is what you want? When you wake up in the morning, will you regret your decision and feel ashamed of what we did?" He raised her hands to his lips. "I never want to be one of your regrets. I never want you to be ashamed of making love with me. You do not have to give your body to me to make me like you." He pulled her closer and cupped her cheek. "I'd like everything about you without ever making love with you."

"Believe me when I say, I want to make love with you, for me. Not to make you like me better." She smiled. "Being with you this past couple of days, I've never felt more comfortable being myself. At the same time, I've never felt so incredibly attracted to someone as I am to you." She tipped her head toward the digital clock on the nightstand. "I want to make love with you...for me. If you still want to make love with me, we'd better get started."

Teller chuckled as he lowered his head and claimed her lips.

She opened to him and met his tongue with her own, thrusting and caressing in sync with him. Then she slid her hands beneath his T-shirt and ran them across his torso.

He leaned back, tore the shirt over his head and flung it across the room.

Sachie followed his lead, removing hers to reveal she wasn't wearing a bra. Her breasts were the perfect size to fit nicely in his palms. He cupped them and softly pinched her nipples until they formed tight little beads.

He bent to capture one in his mouth and flicked the tight button with the tip of his tongue.

Sachie's head rolled back; her fingers weaved into his hair and tugged him closer.

Teller swept her up into his arms and laid her across the bed. He backed up a step and shed his shorts. His staff sprang free.

Sachie scrambled out of her shorts and panties and made room for him on the bed.

Instead of lying beside her, he spun toward the nightstand where he'd left his wallet, praying he had his emergency protection stashed inside. It had been a long time since he'd needed it. He wasn't sure.

When his fingers felt the smooth wrapping, he breathed a relieved sigh and joined Sachie on the bed.

Lying naked beside her, he leaned up on an elbow and brushed his thumb along her jaw. "You're allowed to change your mind, you know."

"Why?" She frowned up at him. "Are you having second thoughts?"

He pressed his lips to hers in a light kiss. "Never."

Her frown disappeared, her hands laced behind

his neck and she said, "Then make love to me like there's no tomorrow."

Teller's eyes narrowed. "You know something I don't?"

Her lips twisted. "Oh, for the love of—" She cupped his chin and stared hard into his eyes. "A little less talk, a little more action."

# CHAPTER 16

TELLER TOUCHED NEARLY every inch of Sachie's body, kissing and tonguing his way across each breast and down her torso until he reached the juncture of her thighs.

By then, she was on fire, her nerves tingled, and she wanted him inside her so badly, she thought that if he didn't get there soon, she might spontaneously combust.

He settled his big body between her legs and draped her thighs over his shoulders.

The position left her vulnerable to whatever he wanted to do, which was at once scary and incredibly exciting.

His thumbs parted her folds as he blew a warm stream of air over her heated clit.

Sachie's breath caught in her throat as she waited for his next move.

A flick of his tongue made her gasp, and her back arched off the bed.

Another flick, and she reached for his hair, her fingers holding him there as he flicked and nipped at that nubbin of delight, sending incredible sensations shooting through her body.

She writhed beneath him and moaned softly.

For a moment, he paused. "You okay?" he asked, his breath warm on her sex.

Forcing air past constricted vocal cords, she managed, "Yes. Oh, yes."

His chuckle warmed her heart while his tongue set her on fire, working her up to the very edge. But he didn't stop until she catapulted over the top. Even then, he continued to flick, suck and lave her clit as she rode the exquisite wave of her release all the way to the very end.

Sachie collapsed against the mattress, breathing hard, still trembling from her release.

Teller climbed up the bed beside her and pulled her into his arms.

Confused, she frowned. "Wait. That's not all, is it?"

He kissed her gently. "We don't have to go any further. I don't want you to feel obligated to do anything."

She leaned back, frowning. "Feel obligated? What the hell are you talking about? Obligation is not what I'm feeling. What I'm feeling is that was just the beginning. Please tell me you're not stopping here. I want more." Maybe her anger was an extension of her desire, because she was fired up and ready to take charge of her own satisfaction.

She leaned up and pushed Teller onto his back. "What happened to me in the past is just that...in the past. I want to make love with you. Not for you to give me an orgasm and be done." Sachie mounted him, planting her knees on either side of him and started lowering herself over his thick, hard erection.

"Aren't you forgetting something?" Teller held up the packet he'd fished out of his wallet.

Sachie snatched it from his fingers, tore it open and scooted down his thighs. Then she rolled the condom over his cock, her hands working it all the way down. She fondled his balls for a moment before getting back to what she wanted, what she desired.

Him.

All of him.

Filling the emptiness inside. Making her feel special and amazing, not dirty and disgusting.

She rose over him and lowered herself onto him, taking his length into her slick channel. She was in control, going after what mattered to her. Instead of feeling dread at the way his body responded to hers, she felt powerful. She'd made him feel that way. Made him desire her.

And he liked her for who she was—all of her, despite her sordid past.

ELLE JAMES

She rocked up on her knees and back down, increasing the speed and intensity with every pass.

Teller's hands gripped her hips, guiding, not forcing.

His body tensed beneath her, his fingers digging into her hips as he thrust upward to meet her downward momentum. Then he tightened his hold, bringing her down on him and holding her there, his face tight, his cock throbbing his release inside her.

For a long moment, he held her hard against him until his body finally relaxed.

Sachie lay down on him, her breasts pressed to his naked chest. She loved the way his chest hairs tickled her skin.

Teller's arms came up around her, his hands smoothing across her back.

Sachie rested her cheek against his neck and inhaled his fresh scent, committing it to memory. Just because they'd made love once didn't mean it would happen again. They'd only known each other for two days. Teller might not be looking for a long-term relationship.

For that matter, Sachie had never considered one, happily resigning herself to the single life.

Until Teller Osgood had burst into her life. Now, she was reevaluating her so-called happy solitude and coming up short.

Not wanting to spoil the moment dwelling on a future she couldn't predict, Sachie gratefully remained where she was, content to stay there as long as she could.

A loud rumble sounded beneath her.

"Was that your stomach?" she asked.

"Yes, ma'am," he said.

She leaned up on her hands and frowned down at him. "You're hungry." A statement, not a question. Her belly rumbled as if in response to his. "We haven't eaten since Ule's breakfast burritos. You must be starved."

"I don't need food when I have you." Teller pulled her back on top of him.

A moment later, his stomach rumbled again, and hers did, too.

She laughed and slid off him onto the bed. "I'm hungry, too."

"They have a great restaurant in the hotel. We could dress and go down for a bite," he suggested.

"Or we could call for room service," she said.

"I like that idea," he said, sitting up. "We can have dinner in bed and be creative for dessert." He grinned and waggled his eyebrows wickedly.

Warmth spread through her at his words. Maybe their lovemaking wouldn't be just a one-and-done event. Her heart filled with hope.

The voice at the back of her mind warned her not to get too attached to the man.

Sachie pushed the negativity even further back in her mind—at least for the moment. They had a dangerous mission ahead of them. She'd let herself dare to hope for more. She'd come back to reality soon enough.

Teller placed the order. While they waited, they dressed in some of the clothes they planned to wear to the biker bar later, holding off on the doo rags they'd use to cover their hair, the leather, fingerless black gloves and the spiked collars.

Without the accessories, they looked like a couple who preferred wearing monochrome outfits in their black shirts and black jeans. Serviceable, but not inspiring.

Well, Teller would inspire all in black. He wore his jeans well with his tight ass and muscular thighs. And he was completely badass with his black T-shirt stretched across his broad chest.

When a knock sounded on the door, Teller went to answer, checking through the peephole first. "The food's here," he said as he released the chain, twisted the deadbolt and pressed the door handle down.

The door exploded inward, knocking Teller backward. He staggered and righted himself in time to block a blow from a man wearing a hotel staff member's shirt over leather pants.

Another man stood behind the first, unable to get past the two men blocking the narrow entryway, throwing punches.

Sachie searched nearby for anything she could use as a weapon against the attackers. She grabbed the ceramic lamp on the nightstand and yanked its cord out of the wall. The lamp was bulky and unwieldy, but it would have to do since the only other option was the remote control. It wouldn't even put a dent in the wall, much less in someone's head.

Teller ducked and jabbed, landing some punches where it counted and taking some that made Sachie wince.

If she could get close enough without getting in Teller's way, she could slam the lamp over the man's head.

She inched up behind the Teller, dancing backward when he backed away and moving forward when he advanced on his attacker.

When the man pulled a knife, Sachie's heart stuttered.

Teller dodged several swipes of the blade and suddenly grabbed the wrist of the hand holding the knife.

"Get back!" he yelled.

Sachie scampered backward with her lamp as Teller dropped onto his back, pulling the man with him. Then he flipped the guy over his head.

The attacker lost his grip on the knife as he crashed into the dresser and landed flat on his back at Sachie's feet.

Before the asshole could catch his breath, Sachie slammed the lamp down on his head.

The man lay still, unmoving.

Teller was back on his feet, fighting the second man. They tumbled into the bathroom, out of Sachie's sight. When she started forward to help, the guy on the floor groaned.

Sachie shoved the guy hard, rolling him over onto his stomach. Quickly, while he was still out of it, she brought his hands behind his back. His arms were heavily tattooed, and one of his hands had the pyramid with the eye inked in black. She tied his wrists together with the lamp cord, cinching it as tight as she could. Then she ripped a sheet off the bed and hurried toward the bathroom.

Teller flew through the door into the narrow entrance, his back slamming into the closet doors. His attacker, a bigger guy than Teller, leaped out and grabbed Teller by the throat.

Teller pushed his hands up between the man's arms, knocking them away. Then he grabbed the man behind the head and shoved him downward. At the same time, he jerked his knee up, slamming it into the guy's nose.

The big guy staggered backward toward Sachie.

She flung the sheet like a net over his head and yanked hard.

The big guy toppled backward and landed on his buddy, struggling to free his head and face from the sheet.

Sachie leaped up onto the bed, out of reach of the man's waving hands. She snagged the bag of biker accessories and her purse, then dropped to the floor and ran.

Teller threw open the door. Once she'd gone through, he followed her out into the hall.

As she turned toward the elevator, two men stepped out, dressed in black leather. They turned to the right, studying the room number direction signs.

Making a split-second decision, Sachie grabbed Teller's hand, leaned against his shoulder and spun away from the elevator. Walking quickly, they moved in the opposite direction from the two men. Sachie lazily swung the bag like they were a honeymooning couple just getting back from shopping. When they reached the end of the hall, Sachie glanced over her shoulder.

The two men had realized they were headed in the wrong direction and started back toward the elevator.

Teller paused at the last hotel room door on the floor, pressed Sachie's back to the door and leaned in for a kiss. "Ready?" he whispered.

She kissed him first and then nodded.

Teller took her hand and ran for the stairwell.

As they burst through the door, they heard a shout behind them and footsteps pounding down the hallway.

In the lead, Sachie raced down the stairs, sometimes taking two at a time or jumping over the last two steps at each landing.

Teller was right behind her.

They'd made it down two flights when the stairwell door above slammed open. Heavy footsteps thundered down the concrete and metal stairs.

Sachie moved faster, praying she didn't lose her footing.

When she reached the bottom of the stairwell, she shoved open the door leading into the lobby. Teller grabbed her hand and led her to the rear of the building, pushing through a door into an empty conference room. They ran past stacks of chairs and tables to the opposite end and through another door. This one led into what Sachie assumed was the staff area used when staging decorations and catering. Eventually, they found an exit onto a loading ramp.

Teller jumped down, reached back, and swung Sachie to the ground. Keeping to the shadows of the building or the landscaping, they worked their way around to the front entrance and watched from their hiding place.

The four men in black leather and tattoos exited the hotel, climbed onto their motorcycles and roared away.

Sachie was happy to wait another five minutes before leaving their hiding place. Then, they hurried toward the car, slid in and drove away from the fancy hotel where they'd spent a beautiful evening making love.

"That was close," Sachie said.

Teller nodded, his face bruised, his bottom lip busted. "Too close. What I wonder is how they knew where to find us?"

"Seriously," Sachie agreed. "We went all over the place today with no problem."

"Until we went to the Boys' Club," Teller said.

"And the guy snatched my purse." Sachie frowned and reached for her purse, which she'd dropped on the floorboard. She found the button for the overhead light and switched it on. Then she removed the contents one at a time, inspected them and dropped them into the accessories bag. She checked every compartment and pocket. At the bottom of the slot she used to hold her sunglasses, she found a small metal disk. "What the hell is this?"

Teller glanced at what she was holding, and his lips pressed into a tight line. "If I'm not mistaken, that's a tracker."

Sachie's stomach dropped. "Son of a bitch."

"Yeah, no kidding," Teller agreed.

"If the rest of the gang is that friendly at the Leather & Chains bar," Sachie said, "we might have to rethink our approach."

# CHAPTER 17

TELLER SAT behind the wheel of the rental car, hesitant to shut off the engine but knowing he had to. They'd arrived just after dark in a beat-up clunker Ingram had secured for the operation. The body looked like hell, but the engine, tires and suspension would get them wherever they wanted to go.

He had parked at an angle from the entrance, far enough back they wouldn't draw attention, but close enough to see every man entering. Prepared to wait, they could be there for an hour, two, or maybe more. He sighed and turned off the engine. "Rogue 2 in position," he said into his mic.

"Roger," Johnson replied. "Rogue 1 in place."

"Roger," Teller said.

Sachie glanced his way, touching a hand to her ear where they'd equipped her with a radio earbud. She looked pretty badass all in black with her blond hair tucked up in a black and gray do-rag and heavy eyeliner ringing her eyes. However, looks weren't everything. She didn't have the body mass and combat training the rest of his team had acquired over their years in special operations.

"I don't feel good about this plan," Teller admitted.

"I'm not feeling all warm and fuzzy myself." Sachie reached across the console for Teller's hand. "But we're not going into the bar, as was the original plan. After I identify Travis, we can leave and let your guys wait for him to leave, follow him to a more secure location, grab him and take him down to the police station. They can question him and get his confession as the arsonist who burned down my office on the Big Island and everything else he's done as my stalker."

"And if he denies all of it?" Teller asked.

"At least he's off the street and will be sent back to jail for violating his parole," Sachie said. "He can't hurt Candice anymore."

"Until he's released on parole again," Teller said.

"Hopefully, that won't be for a long time." Sachie's lips thinned. "And if he isn't my stalker, we've eliminated one suspect."

Teller stared at the entrance to the Leather & Chains bar, wondering if the dull yellow bulb hanging over the door would shed enough light to allow Sachie to pick Travis out of the other patrons who might stop in for a drink. Hell, they weren't even sure Travis would appear that night. His team might be wasting their time and risking their lives for nothing.

"You know, if I were on the run from the law, I wouldn't show my face in any public place," Sachie said. "What if Travis doesn't show up tonight?"

Teller shrugged. "Then we find a different hotel and get some rest."

"Are you sure your guys will be okay inside that place?" A frown creased Sachie's forehead. "I'd hate for them to get hurt on my account."

When Teller and Sachie had met with Ingram, Bennet, Atkins and Johnson, they'd discussed the plan, agreeing that Sachie shouldn't go into the bar, but stay in the car, identify Travis and leave. George Ingram, one of the largest men on the Brotherhood Protectors Hawaii team at six feet four inches, had insisted on going into the bar. Reid Bennet had accompanied him.

The two inside men had dressed in black jeans, leather vests, army boots and do-rags. Neither man had shaved that day and sported thick stubble on their chins. They'd gone to a tattoo parlor to have temporary tattoos airbrushed on their arms, chests and necks. Their broad chests and thick biceps would be enough to make club members think twice about fucking with them. At least, Teller hoped their disguises would do the trick.

"If they get hurt, it wouldn't be your fault," Teller assured Sachie.

"I know," she said, waving a hand. "I won't have pulled the trigger or thrown the punch, but it's because of me that you and your team are here."

"We're here because this is what we do." Teller's fingers tightened around hers. "We protect people."

"But how many of your guys does it take to protect one woman?" Sachie asked. "And how is infiltrating a biker bar protecting me? To me, it seems like overkill, or maybe I'm pushing too hard for too much."

Teller raised her hand to his lips and kissed her knuckles. "We'll be all right as long as we get you out of here unscathed." Her safety was his number one priority. If that meant losing Travis, so be it.

Five tricked-out motorcycles roared into the parking lot. Three of the five had long ape-hanger handlebars. The other two had black and red flames painted across their fuel tanks. Their riders lined up in front of the building and dismounted. Two of the five men had goatee beards. They all had tattoos from the tips of their fingers up their arms and across their necks. None wore helmets, and they all looked as if they chewed nails for fun.

As far as Teller could see, they weren't packing handguns but were probably armed with some lethal knives. The backs of their leather vests had BANDIDOS written in bold letters.

Sachie stared at the group through the mini binoculars Ingram had brought along with the communications equipment and an assortment of weapons, including sheathed knives, switchblades, stun guns and mace.

Sachie lowered the binoculars. "None of them are Travis."

Teller tapped the mic on his headset. "Five Bandidos entering. No bogey."

"Roger," Ingram responded softly.

"Any problems yet?" Teller asked.

"Not so far," Ingram said. "The place was pretty empty when we arrived."

Rex Johnson and Logan Atkins arrived in a truck and parked at the opposite end of the building from Teller's position.

"Rogue 3 in position," Johnson said into their headsets.

"Roger," Johnson replied.

Twenty minutes passed before two bikers arrived on Harleys with DEVILS BREED embroidered across the backs of their vests.

"They like announcing their affiliation, don't they?" Sachie murmured. "Not Travis."

The bikers entered the bar.

As the hour grew later, bikers came and went, more coming than leaving. So far, according to Sachie, not one of them was Travis Finkel.

"I feel like we're wasting time here," Sachie said.

"The man is a parole violator. Surely, even he isn't dumb enough to show up somewhere public."

"Given his criminal record, I wouldn't consider him one of the brightest," Teller said. "It won't hurt us to stay until the place closes. He might choose to come later to avoid the main crowd of bikers."

Sachie nodded and lifted her binoculars to her eyes as a single motorcycle pulled into the parking lot. This bike was different from the others as it was shiny with no distinguishing artwork. Most of the bikers had added saddlebags, fancy handlebars, art or stickers to their rides. Not this one.

"That's a Harley Davidson, and it has a just-driven-off-the-lot look to it," Teller commented.

Sachie tensed beside him, her gaze fixed on the man dismounting. He was one of a handful of men wearing helmets that night. The helmet was black with a dark visor shielding his face. Dressed in faded jeans and a black leather vest with a Harley Davidson logo emblazoned across the back, the man unbuckled the helmet and pulled it off.

Sachie gasped. "That's him."

Teller's eyes narrowed as he studied the biker. "You're sure?"

She nodded. "It's those thick eyebrows. I remember thinking he looked like Javier Bardem, the guy from that movie where he had that awful haircut..."

"*No Country for Old Men*," Teller studied the man.

He did resemble the actor who'd won an Oscar for that part. "The Bogey has landed," Teller said into his mic. "Big guy looks like Javier Bardem."

"The guy with the bad hair in *No Country for Old Men?*" Ingram clarified.

"You got it," Teller confirmed.

"We'll take it from here," Ingram said. "Get out of here."

"Roger," Teller said.

Before he could start the engine, a dozen motorcycles streamed into the already full parking lot.

As they parked wherever they could, they surrounded the car where Teller and Sachie watched and waited.

Teller sank into his seat, his hand on the ignition switch, ready to set the engine in motion should any trouble erupt.

One of the men who'd parked near the front of the building slipped off his bike and turned his face enough that Teller could see the bruised cheekbone of one of the men who'd attacked him in the hotel. "Shit," he whispered. "The guy by my door is one I fought with at the hotel."

Sachie ducked low in her seat as a man strode past her door. She drew in a sharp breath. "That's the guy I hit with the lamp."

Teller didn't dare turn on the engine and draw attention to them. Not until the group of bikers entered the building.

ELLE JAMES

On the backs of their leather vests were the words PELE MAKA.

"Pele Maka," Teller whispered. "Is that Hawaiian for something?"

"Yes," Sachie said. "Pele is the goddess of fire and volcanoes. Maka is the word for eye." She leaned forward, her gaze on a young man climbing off a small motorcycle that looked more like a racing bike or what Teller would have called a "crotch rocket."

The guy's face and the way he wore his hair were familiar.

"Isn't that—" Sachie frowned.

"—the guy who stole your purse," Teller said through clenched teeth. "He didn't stay in jail long."

"The kid with him..." Sachie sucked in a sharp breath, and her face blanched. "Luke," she said, barely above a whisper.

Before Teller knew what was happening, Sachie flung open her door, lunged out of the car and raced for the kid.

"Sachie, no!" Teller cried out. He shoved open his door and leaped out of the car, too late to stop her from following the kid into the building.

Teller's cry had the eight remaining bikers still standing in the parking lot turning toward him.

The man with the bruised cheek pointed at Teller and yelled, "Get the bastard!"

Teller ran for the entrance to the bar, desperate to get to Sachie. He only made it ten feet before the bikers closed ranks around him. A man stepped in front of him and shoved him backward.

Another shoved him from behind, sending him toward the guy with the bruised cheek.

Outnumbered eight to one, Teller would have to fight his way through them to get to Sachie. He balled his fists and came out swinging.

THE NIGHTMARES, the hallucinations and the shadowy sightings of a dead teenager had rushed over Sachie when she'd spotted Luke.

She was out of the car and bursting through the door of the Leather & Chains bar before logic kicked in and slowed her steps.

Luke was dead. The young man she'd seen in the parking lot and followed into the bar couldn't be Luke.

Then she saw him again. The thief who'd taken her purse was shoving the Luke look-alike toward a hallway near the rear of the bar.

Sachie lowered her head and weaved her way through burly bikers smelling of leather, booze and cigarette smoke. She had to know the truth. Who was this kid who looked so much like Luke?

"Hey, chickie, where ya goin' in such a hurry?" A man grabbed her arm. "Stick around. Let me buy you a drink."

She forced a smile and shook her head. "Sorry. Gotta pee. Maybe after?"

"Countin' on it," he said and released her arm. "Don't make me come lookin' for you."

"Wouldn't dream of it." Sachie hurried toward the hallway where the kid and the thief had disappeared. She'd just entered the dark corridor when the thief stepped out of the men's restroom and blocked her path, a sneer pulling his lip up on one side. "I got a grand waiting for me out the back door. All I gotta do is deliver, and bitch, you're making it too easy."

The thief gripped her shoulders.

On instinct, Sachie slammed her palm into his nose.

His hands on her arms loosened enough that Sachie knocked them away, and she ducked around his side.

She'd only gone two steps when he snagged her do-rag, and the hair beneath it, and yanked her to a halt so fast, she fell backward into him, knocking him flat on his back.

Sachie rolled to the side, scrambled to her feet and ran into another set of arms. When she looked up into the face of her captor, all the air left her lungs. "Luke."

"No," said the teen with the dark curly hair and green eyes that looked just like Luke's. "I'm Mark."

"Oh, my God," she said. "You're the twin."

The thief rose to his feet. "Good. You caught her. I'll take her from here."

Mark pushed Sachie behind him. "Can't let you do that."

The thief's eyes narrowed. "Should have known you'd double-cross me. Think you're going to get that thousand all for yourself, then you better think again." The thief launched himself at Mark like a linebacker going in for a tackle.

The teen stepped to the side at the last second and shoved the thief into the wall, headfirst.

The thief sank to his knees and fell onto his side.

Mark hooked Sachie's arm. "You need to get out of here. The Pele Maka are after you." As he turned her back toward the bar, the rear exit door opened.

A man dressed in black jeans and a black leather jacket stepped through. "Mark, Miss Moore? What are you doing here?"

Sachie blinked. "Officer Roland?"

"Yes, it's me," he said, a frown denting his forehead. "This isn't a safe place for you two."

A loud crash sounded from the barroom, and shouts echoed off the rafters.

Roland glanced over their heads. "All hell is breaking loose out front. You can't go that way. If you come with me now, I can get you out the back." He waved them toward him.

The shouting became a roar from the barroom.

Sachie had to get out of the building and back around to the front where Teller and his team were.

Two bikers, locked in each other's arms, bounced off a wall and into the corridor, landing on top of the unconscious thief.

Sachie leaped out of the way and ran toward the rear exit, with Mark behind her.

As soon as they were through the door, Roland followed, pulling the door closed behind him.

Outside, the shouts from within were muffled. But more shouts sounded from the other side of the building.

Officer Roland ran to a nondescript dark sedan and yanked open the back door. "Quick, get into my service vehicle and duck low. You don't want the gang members to see you. You have a price on your head."

As Sachie bent to climb in, Mark grabbed her arm and yanked her back. "Don't."

"But they'll see me." Sachie tugged on her arm, but Mark wouldn't let go. "I need to get back to my car."

"Hurry, Sachie," Roland said, standing on the other side of the door, ready to close it as soon as they got inside. "Get in. I'll get you there." He started to go around the door.

Mark stepped between Sachie and Roland. "Don't go with him."

Sachie laid a hand on Mark's arm. "You heard the officer, I have a price on my head."

"Mark, think before you speak." Roland's voice had changed from desperately helpful to stern and menacing.

Mark stared into Roland's eyes. "Ms. Moore, you have a price on your head because he put it there."

"I warned you. Now, you and the girl will pay." Roland pulled a gun out of his pocket and aimed it at Mark.

Sachie shoved the open car door as hard as she could, hitting Roland's arm as he pulled the trigger.

A loud bang sounded.

Mark jerked sideways and fell to the ground.

"No!" Sachie dropped down beside the teen.

Before she could check for a pulse, she was lifted off the ground and flung into the backseat of the car.

She fought and kicked, landing a foot in Roland's face.

As he reeled backward, cursing, Sachie lunged out of the car.

Roland's arm shot out, catching her around the middle. He pulled her back against his chest and pressed his handgun to her temple. "Stop moving or I'll shoot."

# CHAPTER 18

S<small>URROUNDED BY EIGHT BIKERS</small>, Teller fought like a crazed man, swinging his fists as fast as he could. He caught one guy in the eye, another in the gut and had cocked his arm to go after the man with the bruise when his arms were caught on either side by two hulking men.

Though he fought to be free, they held tight.

The bruised guy came toward him, his lips pulled back in a feral snarl. "You got this coming to you, asshole."

With the big guys holding on so tightly, Teller waited until the bruised guy was in range. Then he lifted both legs and kicked as hard as he could right in the man's bruised face, sending him flying backward.

The men holding him loosened their grasp just

enough for Teller to drop to the ground, roll out of range and pop to his feet.

The seven men still standing closed in on him.

"Hey, Teller," a voice called out.

Atkins and Johnson came at the circle from opposite sides.

"Need a hand cleaning up?" Atkins asked, his expression casual, almost amused.

"Would hardly think it fair, three of us against eight little guys," Teller said, assuming the same amused look while inside his thoughts were screaming to get this done and find Sachie before she got hurt.

"We'll take that as a yes," Johnson said and flipped open a wicked-looking switchblade.

Five of the men in the circle spun to face the new threat.

Teller took on the other two, knocking one out with a side kick to his throat.

When the other pulled out a knife, Teller dodged several jabs and grabbed the man's wrist, ducked behind him and brought the wrist with him, shoving it deep up between his shoulder blades. Then he shoved the man forward and into the middle of a row of motorcycles. He fell over the top of one, taking it down, and, like dominoes, the rest of the motorcycles toppled, trapping the man beneath them.

Teller glanced over his shoulder at Johnson and Atkins. They were down to fighting one biker each.

"Go!" Johnson yelled. "Bennet and Ingram have their hands full. Find Sachie!"

Teller didn't wait for Johnson to finish talking. He ran into the bar.

A fight had broken out between the Bandidos and the Devil's Breed motorcycle clubs. Ingram and Bennet were busy trying to get a zip-tied Travis Finkel past two of the Pele Maka Club members.

Though they looked like they could use help, Teller couldn't stop until he found Sachie.

With so many people fighting, Teller couldn't see through the melee. He headed for the bar, jumped up on the counter and searched feverishly. Sachie was nowhere to be seen in the barroom. He dropped down from the bar and ran for the hallway leading to the restrooms and a back exit.

He'd just poked his head into the ladies' room when he heard the muffled sound of a gunshot. Realizing it was too muffled to be from inside the bar, he ran for the rear exit and burst through in time to find a man dressed in black, holding Sachie with a gun pressed to her temple.

Teller's heart dropped to the pit of his belly. He took in a steadying breath and forced himself to remain calm.

As he studied the man, he realized it was the cop from the station—the same one who volunteered at the Boys' Club.

"Let her go," Teller spoke as calmly and firmly as

he could when he was freaking out inside. The man had his finger on the trigger. If he got the least bit nervous, he might squeeze.

"Stand back," the officer said. "Ms. Moore is under arrest for the murder of Mark Bradford." He tipped his head toward the body on the ground near their feet.

"He's lying," Sachie said. "Officer Roland shot Mark when he tried to help me."

"She took my gun and shot the boy, like she killed his twin in her office," Roland said. "I'm taking her in."

"You're not taking her anywhere." Teller walked toward the officer, taking one step at a time.

"Stay back," Roland shouted. "She's dangerous, I tell you. One step closer, and I'll shoot you for aiding and abetting a felon." The officer moved the hand holding the gun and aimed it at Teller's chest.

Sachie's eyes widened and then narrowed.

"Now, it all makes sense," she said. "You're the one who was pressuring Luke to do something he didn't want to do."

Roland turned the gun back on Sachie's temple. "You don't know what you're talking about. You're the one who killed Luke and made it look like suicide. And now, you've killed his brother."

"It's over, Alan," she said.

"For you," he said. "You tried to escape. Your boyfriend tried to help you. I warned you to stop."

Teller moved closer. Officer Roland was quickly losing touch with reality. If he didn't do something soon...

Suddenly, Sachie's entire body sagged, and her chin dipped toward her chest as if she'd passed out.

Officer Roland struggled to hold her up with one arm, her deadweight making him stagger forward, the gun in his other hand tipped away from her temple.

Teller lunged forward.

At the same time, Sachie slammed her head backward, smashing into Officer Roland's nose.

The gun went off a split second before Teller grabbed the officer's wrist and shoved it skyward.

Roland released Sachie and fought for control of the gun, squeezing off another round.

Teller rammed into the police officer, sending him backward until he crashed into the car behind him.

Sirens wailed in the distance, getting louder as they got closer.

His patience at an end, Teller channeled all his strength and anger into his hands and slammed Roland's wrist into the hard metal of the car, again and again, until he let go of the gun, and it fell to the ground.

Once the gun was out of Roland's hand, Teller spun him around and shoved his wrist up between his shoulder blades, the anger still burning in his blood. He wanted to slam the man's face into the car and would have if not for the hand on his shoulder.

"Teller," Ingram's voice sounded close by. "He's not worth it. Let the court decide his fate."

"This man almost killed the woman I love," Teller whispered.

"All the more reason to let him live. The woman isn't going to be interested in you if you're behind bars." Ingram tapped his shoulder. "Now that we have Travis, and he's headed back to jail, he's willing to take as many of his buddies with him, including your crooked police officer. Atkins and I will take charge of him. You might want to check on your girl."

Johnson and Atkins secured Roland with one of his own zip ties.

Teller spun to find Sachie kneeling on the ground beside the young man she'd followed into the bar. She'd removed the do-rag from her hair and pressed it against the wound on the teen's belly. "He's got to live," she said, tears streaming from her eyes.

"I'm not...going...anywhere," Mark whispered. "Must...testify...even if...I go...to...jail. Can't let...him...go...free. He'll hurt...Luke's..." the teen's eyes closed, "...friend."

"Mark?" Sachie called out. "Stay with me."

Teller pressed his fingers to the base of the teen's throat. "He's got a pulse, and he's breathing."

The police arrived, followed by an ambulance.

The emergency medical technicians took over,

loaded Mark into the ambulance and rushed him to the hospital.

The police took Alan Roland, Travis Finkel and the purse thief into custody. They held the members of the Pele Maka motorcycle club until a paddy wagon arrived to transport them to jail.

As the dust settled and the parking lot cleared, the Brotherhood Protectors gathered around. Teller slipped an arm around Sachie's waist and held her close.

"I've got Hawk and Patterson on speaker." Ingram held out his phone.

"Hawk, here," Jace Hawkins said. "I hear from the Hawaii Police that you managed to reveal a bad player on the police force."

"And if that wasn't enough," Hank Patterson's voice came on, "my contacts in the DEA report that your work tonight put a major kink in the flow of drugs from the Sinaloa Cartel out of Mexico. Excellent work."

Teller smiled down at Sachie. "Couldn't have done it without one feisty shrink head-butting the man calling the shots and running the drugs through the Pele Maka gang and the Boys' Club."

"Travis Finkel, one of Officer Roland's thugs, was happy to throw one of Honolulu's finest under the bus on his way back to federal prison," Ingram said.

"Officer Roland had a network of distributors in the Pele Maka gang as well as teens he recruited at the Boys' Club using strong-arm tactics if they weren't lured by money."

"In Luke's case, he was threatening to hurt Luke's friend if he didn't fall in line and deal drugs," Sachie said. "Luke probably figured if he wasn't in the picture, they wouldn't hurt his friend." Her brow wrinkled. "Mark also said Roland would hurt Luke's friend." She looked up at Teller. "Could they both have meant Luke's girlfriend, Kylie?"

Teller's head tilted and his eyes narrowed. "Makes sense."

"I heard from the hospital," Hawk said. "Mark Bradford was rushed into surgery immediately. He's already out and stable in the ICU. They're optimistic he'll have a full recovery."

Sachie leaned her face into Teller's leather vest. "Thank God."

"Great job," Hawk said. "You're an amazing team."

"I agree," Patterson said. "Thanks for being a part of the Brotherhood Protectors."

"Now, get some rest," Hawk said. "Teller and Ms. Moore, Mr. Parkman has a penthouse suite at the Hilton Hawaiian Village. He's sent word to them to put you up for the next three nights while Ms. Moore's cottage is being repaired and an alternate location is secured for her counseling practice. Kalea wants you to relax and feel better about coming back to the Big Island. But she said she'd understand if you choose to stay on Oahu."

"That's very nice of Kalea and Mr. Parkman," Sachie said.

"My wife would understand if you stayed on Oahu," Hawk said, "but I'm selfish. I want you to stay on the Big Island because it would make my wife happy. And a happy wife makes a happy life."

Johnson coughed at the same time as he said, "Henpecked."

"I heard that," Hawk said. "Wait until you have a wife who's eight months pregnant with your baby. You'll be singing a different tune."

"Not going to happen," Johnson said. "Can't have a wife if you don't get married. I'm not getting married."

"Famous last words," Ingram said. "You just haven't found your person—the one you can't live without."

"She doesn't exist," Johnson said.

"What do you want to bet he's the next one to fall?" Bennet said. "Right after Teller."

Teller frowned. "Hey, give me a minute. Sachie and I just met a few nights ago."

"Man, believe me when I say…" Bennet shook his head, "when you know, you know."

Teller smiled down at Sachie. "Do you know?"

She stared up into his eyes for a long moment and finally nodded.

Teller let out the breath he hadn't known he'd

been holding, gathered her into his arms and held her tightly.

"Yeah, Teller knows," Bennet said. "Come on. Let's leave these two alone. I have my person waiting for me at home, and I can't get there soon enough."

"Same," Ingram said as he walked away with the others.

"Our backup is bailing on us," Teller leaned back and stared down into Sachie's eyes, his heart full to bursting.

"There's a penthouse suite with our names on it," Sachie said. "And I won't hold you to any commitment if you don't know what you know."

He bent to press his lips to hers. "You had me at the point of a butcher knife, all hellfire and grit. And if that wasn't enough, the lamp attack sealed it. You're my person. You're one hundred percent badass, and you'll always have my back."

"And I know you'll never hurt me, and you'll protect me when I can't do it alone." She wrapped her arms around his waist and hugged him close. "I never thought I would want to be as close as I want to be with you. You showed me it's possible in the gentlest way." She looked up at him. "I'm excited to see where life takes us."

Teller turned with her in the crook of his arm and firmly fixed in his heart. "First stop is a penthouse."

# EPILOGUE

*TWO MONTHS LATER...*

Sachie stepped out onto the porch of the Parkman ranch house, followed closely by Teller. She grinned at her friend, Kalea. "He did it. Teller managed to change Kai's diaper all by himself," she said, turning toward the man she loved with all her heart and holding out her hands. "Want me to take her?"

Teller frowned, his arms tightening gently around the infant. "No way. I earned some snuggle time with the nugget." He eased into a rocking chair close to the porch swing where Kalea and Hawk had settled.

"Thank you for pulling diaper duty," Kalea said. "We're so exhausted from lack of sleep, I don't know whether I'm coming or going."

Hawk laughed. "And I thought forty-eight hours on a mission was bad. I'll be glad when Kai is sleeping through the night."

"That's why we're here," Sachie assured the new parents. "Teller and I will take the graveyard shift for a couple of nights so you two can catch up on sleep."

Kalea tipped her head back against Hawk's shoulder and sighed. "You have no idea what that means to us. I still have to nurse her, but it'll be nice to have someone bring her to me, then burp and rock her back to sleep when her tummy's full." She frowned across at Sachie. "Are you sure you have time to do this?"

Sachie leaned against the porch rail, her gaze on Teller and the baby. "I don't usually work with patients on the weekend, so I'm all yours." Her lips twisted. "I do have one online session this evening with one of my patients back on Oahu."

"I'll cover with the baby," Teller quickly volunteered. "She likes her Uncle Teller. See? She's smiling."

"Dude." Hawk chuckled. "At a month old, it's probably gas."

Teller cocked an eyebrow at Kai, lying across his knees. "Are you going to let your daddy talk about you like that?"

The baby cooed.

"Exactly." Teller glanced across at his boss, Hawk. "She says little ladies don't have gas."

Kalea glanced across at Sachie. "I thought you passed your patients back to Dr. Janek when you left Oahu."

"I did. But after all that happened, I gained two online patients." She smiled. "Luke had talked to Mark about his sessions with me. Despite the fact his twin had committed suicide in front of me, Mark wanted me to help him through the aftermath of losing the twin he never knew he had until it was too late. Plus, he wanted guidance on moving forward after finally being free of the pressure Roland put on him to deal drugs."

Kalea shook her head. "How could someone who was sworn to protect, honor and serve on the police force hold so many people in fear?"

"Roland was in the perfect position, unfortunately," Sachie said. "A trusted community servant and a volunteer at the Boys' Club. As an outsider looking in, I never suspected him—and neither did anyone else."

"Well, he'll be behind bars along with Travis Finkel," Hawk said. "Who's the other patient you're seeing as a result of all that happened, if you don't mind sharing?"

"One of the guys we followed, thinking he might be a suspect—Scott Williams. I met with him and his parole officer. I felt it was my responsibility to report that I'd seen him in the park across from his son's school, since he wasn't supposed to be there. When Scott found out I was a mental health counselor, he asked me to help him work to be a better father."

Kalea frowned heavily. "Do you think he'll ever hurt his son like he did before?"

Sachie shook her head. "No. He feels awful about what he did and wants to earn back the love his son had willingly given him. He goes before the court next week to ask for custody." Sachie smiled. "I'm going to give testimony about how far he's come with anger management and learning proper parenting skills." She shot a glance at Teller. "He was hurting when his wife left him and his small son. He knows he should never take his anger out on a child, and he feels huge remorse for having hurt the little guy."

Hawk frowned. "Unfortunately, not everyone is remorseful for the atrocities they inflict on others."

"Sociopaths feel no remorse," Sachie said. "Anyway, if Scott gets custody of his son, I promised him I'd keep him as a patient and make myself available when he needs someone to talk to."

"I heard Hank had a hand in getting Mark a good lawyer," Hawk said. "Mark's depositions against Roland, along with Travis Finkel's, will keep Roland in jail for a long time."

"And the lawyer got Mark's juvenile record expunged," Sachie said with a grin. "He won't have any black marks on his background checks."

"Which is in his favor," Hawk said. "He's signed up to join the Navy upon high school graduation.

George Ingram and Reid Bennet will work with him to ensure he's in top physical condition. The boy wants to be a Navy SEAL."

Teller stared down at the baby lying on his thighs. "We tried to talk him into going Army and Delta Force, didn't we, Kai?"

"What can I say?" Hawk spread his hands wide. "The kid chose the right branch of the military."

Teller snorted.

"So," Kalea cocked and eyebrow toward Sachie and then Teller, "you two have been living together for a couple months, what's the verdict? Are you able to stand each other enough to make a commitment?"

Sachie's cheeks burned. She shot a glance toward Teller. "Can we tell them?"

Teller's lips twisted. "I would have told them a week ago, but someone wanted to do it in person." He smiled. "Go ahead."

"You're engaged!" Kalea leaped out of the porch swing and wrapped her arms around Sachie.

Sachie laughed. "Uh, no, not quite," she said.

Kalea frowned and leaned back, not releasing her hold on Sachie. "You're not? Don't tell me you decided you aren't compatible." She shook her head. "Outside of me and Jace, you two are the most amazing couple I know."

Sachie met Teller's gaze.

His eyes sparkled with amusement.

"We got married a week ago in front of a Justice of the Peace." She dug in her pocket, slipped the beautiful white-gold and diamond band onto her ring finger and held it up.

"Oh, no, you didn't!" Kalea's expressions ran the gamut of surprise, happiness, disappointment and then back to happiness. She hugged Sachie close, tears slipping down her cheeks. "I so wanted to be the matron of honor at your wedding."

Sachie returned her friend's hug and brushed a tear from her cheek. "We decided we didn't need a fancy wedding, or a long engagement when we already knew we loved each other from the start."

Teller glanced up from the baby. "When you know, you know. Sachie is my person."

"Like Hawk's mine," Kalea said.

"Only, I had an uphill battle convincing her," Hawk added.

Kalea shrugged and gave him a lopsided grin. "I wasn't fighting against you, sweetie, I was fighting myself. I didn't want a man dictating my life for me."

"And have I?"

Kalea shook her head, a loving smile gracing her lips. "We're partners, lovers and now..." she tipped her head toward Kai, "parents. And I wouldn't have it any other way."

"Except a little more sleep?" Hawk said with a grin.

"There is that." Kalea turned back to Sachie. "But

enough about us, tell me everything. Did you at least get a special dress, and did Teller wear a tux?"

Sachie grinned. "I wore a simple white sundress. Teller wore a gray suit and a black and gray tie. He brought me the most beautiful bouquet of maile leaves, lehua blossoms and orchids. We both wore plumeria leis. The JP's assistant took photos. I'm having an album made up with them. I'll show you when it comes in."

"I want to be sad that I didn't get to be with you, but I'm happy if you're happy," Kalea said.

Sachie drew in a deep breath and let it out on a joyous laugh. "I'm happier than I've ever been in my life. Teller is everything and more than I could have dreamed of."

"And you're an amazing, caring woman," Teller said from where he sat, playing with Kai. "I love you, Sachie, more than I thought was possible."

"Oh, you two are so incredibly sweet," Kalea said. Then her eyes widened. "We need to celebrate with champagne." She started for the front door. "Not that I can have any while I'm nursing, but everyone else can."

Sachie caught her arm before she got away. "That's okay. We don't need champagne," she said, her cheeks heating.

"Then a beer or whiskey to toast your wedded bliss," Kalea insisted.

Her cheeks burning, Sachie shook her head. "I can't have alcohol because I'm pregnant."

Kalea froze, turned and stared at Sachie, her jaw dropping. "What? Wait. How? When?" She shook her head as if to clear it.

Sachie laughed. "You know the penthouse your father so graciously offered after we solved the case of my stalker?"

Kalea's eyes widened. "You mean you're two months along and you're just now telling me? Is there anything else you'd like to share?" She flung her hands in the air. "Oh, what does it matter? My friend is married and having a baby." Once again, she engulfed Sachie in a hug.

"Now I understand why Teller insisted on changing Kai's diaper." Kalea wiped tears from her eyes.

Teller smiled at Kalea. "I need all the practice I can get. We'll have our own little nugget in seven months."

"And Kai will have a friend to play with," Kalea sighed, released Sachie and gathered her baby in her arms. "Do you hear that, Kai? You'll have a friend to play with and ride horses with and learn to dance with."

Kai nuzzled against her mother's breast.

"Hungry again?" Kalea laughed and pushed to her feet. "I'd better feed her. But we're not finished with this conversation," As she entered the house, she called out over her shoulder, "Since you didn't let us be a part of your wedding, the least you can do is let us host the reception and baby shower."

"I'd love that," Sachie called out as the door closed behind Kalea.

"I need to check in with Hank and some of the guys before I call it a night," Hawk said. "Congratulations on the marriage and your baby news. I'm happy for you both."

Sachie's gaze followed Hawk as he strode away from the house toward the outbuilding the Brotherhood Protectors used as their Hawaiian headquarters.

Teller joined her at the railing and slipped his arm around her, his hand resting on her flat belly.

She covered his hand with hers. "I can't wait until I can feel our baby move inside me."

"Me, too," Teller said and pressed a kiss to her temple. "I can't believe we're jumping into our life together with both feet."

She glanced up at him, her brow furrowing. "Any regrets?"

He touched his lips to her forehead. "Only one."

Sachie's heart dipped into her belly. "Really?"

He chuckled. "I regret we didn't meet sooner. You showed me how good it could be to love someone. And once I started down that path, I can't stop...loving you."

She leaned back in his arms. "And you showed me

what real love is, through your gentle patience and strength." Sachie turned in his arms. "I love you, Teller, more than I ever thought possible, and I want to be with you for the rest of my life and beyond."

"Good, because I want the same." He kissed her, then leaned back and smiled. "When you know...you know."

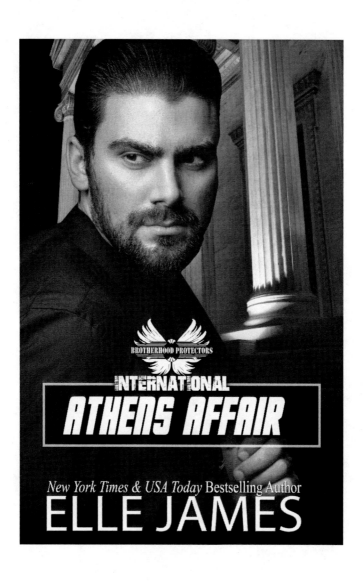

BROTHERHOOD PROTECTORS

INTERNATIONAL

# ATHENS AFFAIR

New York Times & USA Today Bestselling Author

# ELLE JAMES

# ATHENS AFFAIR

BROTHERHOOD PROTECTORS
INTERNATIONAL BOOK #1

*New York Times* & *USA Today*
Bestselling Author

**ELLE JAMES**

# CHAPTER 1

HIRING on with the Jordanian camera crew as their interpreter hadn't been all that difficult. With Jasmine Nassar's ability to speak Arabic in a Jordanian dialect and also speak American English fluently, she'd convinced the Jordanian camera crew she had the experience they needed to handle the job. However, the resume she'd created, listing all the films she'd worked on, had probably lent more weight to their decision.

Not that she'd actually worked on any movie sets. Her ability to "be" anything she needed to be, to fit into any character or role, was a talent she exploited whenever needed since she'd been "released" from the Israeli Sayeret Matkal three years earlier.

Her lip curled. Released was the term her commanding officer had used. *Forced out* of the special forces unit was closer to the truth. All because of an affair she'd had with an American while she'd been on holiday in Greece. Because of that week in Athens, her entire life had upended, throwing her into survival mode for herself and one other—her entire reason for being. The reason she was in Jordan about to steal the ancient copper scroll.

The Americans arrived on schedule for the afternoon's shoot at the Jordan Museum in Amman, Jordan. The beautiful film star Sadie McClain appeared with her entourage of makeup specialists, hairstylists, costume coordinators, and a heavy contingent of bodyguards, including her husband, former Navy SEAL Hank Patterson.

Sadie was in Jordan to film an action-adventure movie. All eyes would be on the beautiful blonde, giving Jasmine the distraction she'd need to achieve her goal.

Much like the movie heroine's role, Jasmine was there to retrieve a priceless antique. Only where Sadie was pretending to steal a third-century BC map, Jasmine was there to take the one and only copper scroll ever discovered. The piece dated back to the first century AD, and someone with more money than morals wanted it badly enough he'd engaged Jasmine to attain it for him.

Up until the point in her life when she'd been driven out of her military career, she'd played by the rules, following the ethical and moral codes demanded by her people and her place in the military. Since the day she'd been let go with a dishonorable discharge, she'd done whatever it took to survive.

She'd been a mercenary, bodyguard, private investigator and weapons instructor for civilians wanting to know how to use the guns they'd purchased illegally to protect themselves from terrorist factions like Hamas.

Somewhere along the way, she must have caught the eye of her current puppet master. He'd done his homework and discovered her Achilles heel, then taken that weakness in hand and used it to make her do whatever he wanted her to do.

And she'd do it because he had her by the balls. He held over her head the one thing that would make her do anything, even kill.

Her contact had timed her efforts with the filming of the latest Sadie McClain blockbuster. The museum was closed to the public that afternoon but was filled with actors, makeup artists, cameramen, directors and sound engineers.

The American director had insisted on an interpreter, though Jasmine could have told him it was redundant as nearly half the population of Jordan spoke English. Part of the deal they'd struck with the Jordanian government had been to employ a certain percentage of Jordanian citizens during the production of the movie. An interpreter was a minor concession to the staffing and wouldn't interfere with the rest of the film crew.

Plus, one inconsequential interpreter wouldn't be noticed or missed when she slipped out with the scroll in hand.

For the first hour, she moved around the museum with the film crew, reaffirming the exits, chokepoints and, of course, the location of her target. She'd visited the museum days before as a tourist, slowly strolling through, taking her time to examine everything about the building that she could access, inside and out.

The scroll was kept in a climate-controlled room away from the main hallways and exhibits. Since the facility was closed to the public, there wouldn't be anyone in the room.

While the crew set up for a scene with Sadie McClain, Jasmine slipped into the room to study the display cases once more.

The copper scroll had been cut into multiple pieces. Each piece had its own display case with a glass top, and each was locked. She'd brought a small file in the crossbody satchel she carried, along with a diamond-tipped glass cutter in the event the locks proved difficult. Cutting glass was the last resort. It would take too much time and could make too much noise if the glass shattered.

She'd honed her skills in picking locks and safe-cracking as a child, one of the many skills her mother had taught her. She'd insisted Jasmine be able to survive should anything ever happen to her parents.

Her mother had been orphaned as a small child in the streets of Athens. To survive, she'd learned to steal food and money, or valuables that could be sold for cash or traded for food.

From picking pockets and swiping food from stores and restaurants, she'd worked her way up to stealing jewelry, priceless antiques and works of art from the rich all around the Mediterranean. She'd used her beauty and ability to quickly learn new languages to her advantage, infiltrating elite societal circles to divest the rich and famous of some of their wealth.

She'd gone from a starving, barefoot child, wearing rags in the streets of Athens, to a beautiful young woman, wearing designer clothes and shoes and moving among the who's who of the elite.

Her life had been what she'd made of it until she'd met Jasmine's father, a sexy, Israeli Sayeret Matkal soldier, at an Israeli state dinner attended by wealthy politicians, businessmen and their wives. She'd just stolen a diamond bracelet from the Israeli prime minister's wife.

The special forces soldier outfitted in his formal uniform had caught her with the diamond bracelet in her pocket and made her give it back as if the woman had dropped it accidentally.

Rather than turn her in for the theft, he'd kept her

close throughout the evening, dancing with her and pretending she was just another guest.

Her mother had fallen for the handsome soldier and agreed to meet him the next day for coffee. Less than a month later, they'd married.

For love, her mother had walked away from her life as a thief to be a wife and mother. But she'd never forgotten the hard lessons she'd learned on the streets. She'd insisted her daughter learn skills that could mean the difference between independence and dying of starvation or being reliant on someone who didn't give a damn about her health or happiness.

Her mother had taught her what school hadn't, from languages, dialects and staying abreast of the news to learning skills like picking locks, safe cracking, picking pockets and hacking into databases for information. She'd learned skills most parents didn't teach their children or warned their children to avoid.

Jasmine had earned her physical capabilities from her father. As an only child, she'd been the son her father never had. As an elite Sayeret Matkal, her father had kept his body in top condition. Jasmine had worked out at home with him and matched his running pace, determined to keep up with the father she loved so fiercely.

He'd taught her how to use a variety of weapons and the art of defending herself when she had no weapons at all. Because of her dedication to conditioning, her hand-to-hand combat skills and her ability to speak multiple languages, when she'd joined the Israeli military, she'd been accepted into Sayeret Matkal training soon after.

After the Athens affair and her subsequent release from the elite forces, she'd continued her training.

Now, due to circumstances out of her immediate control, she was on the verge of stealing from a museum the priceless copper scroll the Jordanians were so proud of.

Her jaw hardened. If she had to steal every last item in the museum, she would—anything to get Eli back alive.

She pulled the file from her satchel, glanced toward the room's entrance and then bent to stick the file into the little keyed lock. She fiddled with the lock until she tripped the mechanism, and the lock clicked open.

Jasmine tested the case top by lifting it several inches and then easing it back down. One down, several more to go. She'd work them a few at a time. When she had all the locks disengaged, she'd take the scroll and walk out of the museum or leave with the Jordanian film crew.

She cringed at the thought of waiting for the crew to head home. They could be there well into the night, filming take after take until they perfected the sequences.

No, she'd head out as soon as she could. She had a deadline she would not miss—could not miss—if she wanted to see Eli again.

Jasmine jimmied the locks on a few more of the displays and then returned to where the crew was staging the next scene with Sadie McClain.

In the shadow of a statue, one of Sadie's bodyguards shifted, his eyes narrowing. He wore a baseball cap, making it difficult to see his face.

Something about the way he held himself, the line of his jaw and the dark stubble on his chin struck a chord of memory in Jasmine. A shiver of awareness washed over her. She hurried past him without making eye contact.

When she looked back, the space where he'd been standing was empty.

Jasmine shook off a feeling of déjà vu and stood near the Jordanian camera crew, interpreting when needed but basically remaining quiet and out of the way.

With the preparations for the big scene complete, the camera crews stood ready for the director to shout *action*.

All other personnel were to move out of the line of sight of the cameras. This gave Jasmine the opportunity to slip back into the room with the copper scroll. When she heard the director shout, *"Action,"* Jasmine went to work quickly and efficiently, lifting the tops off the glass cases one at a time, wrapping each piece of the copper scroll in a soft swatch of fabric she'd brought in her satchel, handling them carefully so as not to break the fragile copper.

Jasmine placed each piece inside a box she'd designed specifically for transporting the delicate scroll. Once all the pieces were stored, she closed the box and slid it into her satchel.

Taking the extra time, she returned all the tops of the glass cases to their original positions so they wouldn't draw attention until a museum employee just happened to notice the cases were empty. That should buy her time to get the items out of the museum and out of Jordan before anyone became suspicious.

With her satchel tucked against her side, Jasmine hurried out of the room. At that moment, the director yelled, "Cut!" He motioned to the film crews and gave orders to the American and Jordanian cameramen.

Some of the Jordanians looked around for their interpreter.

Ready to get the hell out of the museum, Jasmine had no choice but to approach the cameramen and provide the necessary translation for the director. All the while, her hand rested on her satchel, anxiety mounting. The longer she stayed in the museum, the greater the chance of someone discovering the copper scroll was missing.

Short of racing out of the building and drawing

ELLE JAMES

attention to herself, she remained, forcing a calm expression on her face when inside she was ready to scream. A life depended on her getting out of the museum and delivering the scroll—Eli's life.

ACE HAMMERSON—HAMMER back in his Navy days—thought he recognized the interpreter as soon as she'd stepped through the museum doors with the Jordanian camera crew. The more he studied her, the more he was convinced it was her.

*Jasmine.*

The woman with whom he'd spent an amazing week in Athens. A week he could never forget.

Had it really been four years?

Granted, she looked different from the last time he'd seen her. She'd changed. Her dark hair peeked out from beneath the black scarf she wore over her head and draped around her shoulders. Her curves were hidden beneath a long black tunic and black trousers. Her face was a little thinner, but those full, rosy lips and her eyes gave her away. There was no mistaking the moss green irises that had captivated him from the first time he'd met her at an outdoor café in the Monastiraki district of Athens.

He'd come to Antica Café on a recommendation from a buddy who'd been there a year earlier. The place had been packed, with no empty tables left. Tired and hungry after the twenty-hour journey

300

from San Diego to Athens, he'd just wanted to eat, find his hotel and crash.

Rather than look for a less crowded café, he'd looked for an empty seat. A beautiful woman sat in a far corner, a book in her hand, enjoying a cup of expresso. Ace had approached, hoping she wouldn't blow him off, and asked if she spoke English.

She'd looked up at him with those amazing green eyes and smiled. In that moment, he'd felt a stirring combination of lust, longing and... strangely...homecoming wash over him. It could have been exhaustion, but more than hunger made him want to join this woman at her table.

She spoke English with a charming accent he couldn't place as either Greek or Arabic. When he'd asked if he could share her table, she'd tilted her head and stared at him with slightly narrowed eyes before finally agreeing with a relaxed smile.

That had been the beginning of the most incredible week of his life. His only regret was that he'd had to go back to work after that week. Before he'd had time to look her up, based on the phone number she'd given him, he'd deployed for several months to Afghanistan, where the mission had been so secret, they'd gone incommunicado to avoid any leaks.

By the time he'd returned to his home base, her number had been disconnected.

He hadn't known where to begin looking for her. In all their conversations, she'd barely revealed much about her life other than both her parents were dead, having been killed in a Hamas strike in Israel.

Because of her reference to her parents being killed in a Hamas strike, he'd assumed she was from Israel. She'd talked about her mother having been from Greece and her father from Israel. Like him, her father had been on vacation in Athens when he'd met her.

Ace had searched for her online, hoping to find out something about her whereabouts, but failed miserably. On his next vacation, he'd gone back to Greece, to the same restaurant where they'd met, hoping by some strange coincidence he'd find her there. He'd walked the same paths they'd walked through the city, looking for her. He'd stayed in the same hotel where they'd stayed, even insisting on the same room.

She hadn't been there. He'd gone to Tel Aviv and talked with some acquaintances he'd met during joint training exercises with the Israeli military. They hadn't heard of her.

As many people as there were in Israel, Ace hadn't expected to find her just by asking around. But he'd hoped that the same magic that had brought them together the first time would help him find her again. After a year, he'd admitted defeat and tried to forget her.

That had never happened. Every woman he'd dated after Jasmine had never sparked in him the fire and desire he'd felt with the woman he'd met in Athens.

Now, here he was, freshly out of the military, working with Hank Patterson and his team of Brotherhood Protectors in Amman, Jordan. Nowhere near Athens and four years after that fated affair, she walked back into his life.

New to the Brotherhood Protectors, Ace had agreed to accompany Hank and members of his team to Jordan to provide security for the film crew and actors who were friends of Hank's wife, Sadie McClain, on her latest movie set. He'd be an extra, there to observe one of the team's assignments.

They didn't always provide security for film crews, but since significant unrest existed in the countries surrounding the relatively stable Jordan, the film producers and studio had budgeted for a staff of security specialists.

Hank had worked with the studio and cut them a deal to ensure his people provided security for his wife and the crew there to make movie magic. Brotherhood Protectors were the most qualified to provide the safety net they might need if fighting spilled over the borders from countries surrounding Jordan.

Though he'd been excited and curious about the mechanics of making a movie, Ace's attention had shifted the moment Jasmine entered the museum.

His gaze followed her as she moved among the Jordanian film crew, standing between Americans and Jordanians, interpreting instructions when needed.

As the camera crew set up, Jasmine left them to wander around the museum, looking at ancient artifacts on display. At one point, she disappeared into a side room and remained gone for several minutes.

Ace started to follow when Hank approached him. "It's amazing, isn't it?"

Ace nodded. "Yes, sir."

Hank grinned. "I never imagined the amount of people it takes to produce a film until I accompanied Sadie on set for the first time."

Though Ace would rather focus his attention on Jasmine's movements, he gave his new boss all his attention. "I never realized there was so much involved."

"Right? It takes an incredible amount of coordination to set up a gig like this, from securing a location to getting permission, in this case, from the government to film here, to transporting all the equipment. Not to mention hiring people to do all aspects, including lighting, sound, video, makeup and costumes."

Ace's gaze remained on the door through which Jasmine had disappeared. "And that's just the filming," he commented, mentally counting the seconds Jasmine was out of his sight.

Then, she emerged from the room and rejoined her camera crew.

Ace let go of the breath he'd been holding.

Hank continued the conversation Ace had lost track of. "After the filming, there's the editing, music, marketing and more." The former Navy SEAL shook his head, his lips forming a wry smile. "I have so much more respect for all those names that scroll across the screen in the movie theater when they show the credits." He chuckled. "I always wondered, and now I know, what a key grip is."

Jasmine worked with the cameramen once more, then stepped back into the shadows.

Once the cameramen were in place, the lighting guy gave a thumbs-up. The director nodded, spoke with Sadie and then stepped back.

"They're about to start filming," Hank said.

When the director raised a hand, everyone grew quiet.

The director looked around at the placement of the cameras, Sadie and the lighting, then nodded.

Ace felt as though everyone took a collective breath, waiting for it...

"Action!" the director called out.

Ace's attention was divided between Jasmine, the actors, the cameramen and the supporting staff.

The beautiful, blond actress, Sadie McClain, did not command his attention like Jasmine.

Sure, Sadie was gorgeous, dressed in khaki slacks that hugged her hips, boots up to her knees and a flowing white blouse tucked into the narrow waist-band of her trousers.

Her mane of golden hair had been styled into a natural wind-swept look with loose waves falling to her shoulders. She worked her way through the museum corridor, pretending to be a patron until she arrived at a golden statue encased in a glass box.

As Sadie studied the statue, her character assessing her chances of stealing it, Jasmine slipped out of the main museum corridor into the side room again.

What was she doing in there?

Ace wanted to follow her, but to do so, he'd have to pick his way through the camera crews and lighting people. He didn't want to get in the way while the cameras were rolling. God forbid he should trip over a cable, make a noise or cast a shadow and make them have to start all over again.

So, he stood as still as a rock, all his attention on that room, counting the seconds until Jasmine came out or the director called, "Cut!"

Finally, Jasmine emerged from the room.

At the same time, the director yelled, "Cut!"

The crossbody satchel she'd worn pushed behind her now rested against the front of her hip; her hand balanced on it. Her head turned toward the museum entrance and back to the organized chaos of camera crews shifting positions and responding to the director's suggestions. An American cameraman approached the Jordanian crew and spoke in English.

Members of the Jordanian camera crew frowned, looking lost. One of them spotted Jasmine and waved her over.

Jasmine's brow furrowed. Her gaze darted toward the museum entrance once more before she strode across the floor to join the cameramen. She listened to the American cameraman and translated what he was saying for the Jordanians, who, in turn, grinned, nodded, and went to work adjusting angles.

Jasmine stepped back into the shadows.

Ace nodded to Hank. "Excuse me. I want to check on something."

Hank's eyes narrowed as his gaze swept through the people milling about. "Anything to be concerned about?"

Was there anything to be concerned about? Ace's gut told him something was off, but he didn't see a need to alarm Hank until he had a better idea of what. "No, I just want to look at some of the displays."

"Are you a history buff?" Hank asked.

"A little. I'm always amazed at artifacts that were created centuries much earlier than our country's inception."

Hank nodded. "Yeah, some of the items in this museum date back hundreds of years before Christ."

He gave Ace a chin lift. "Explore while you can. It looks like they're getting ready for another take."

His gaze remained on Jasmine as Ace strode across the smooth stone floors to the room Jasmine had visited twice in less than an hour.

The room was climate-controlled, with soft lighting and several display cases positioned at its center. At a brief glance, nothing appeared out of place, but as Ace moved closer to the display cases, he frowned. They appeared...

Empty.

His pulse leaped as he read the information plaque beside the row of cases.

COPPER SCROLL. 1ST CENTURY AD.

He circled the cases and found that they all had keyed locks. He didn't dare lift the tops off the cases. If he did, he'd leave his fingerprints all over the glass and possibly be accused of stealing what had been inside.

His stomach knotted. Jasmine had been in here. Had she come to steal the copper scroll? Did she have it stashed in that satchel she'd carried around all afternoon?

Ace spun on his heels and left the room. His gaze went to the last place he'd seen Jasmine. She wasn't there.

His pulse slammed into hyperdrive as he scanned the vast corridor where the film crew worked.

She was nowhere to be seen.

Ace strode toward the museum's entrance. As he neared the massive doors, someone opened the door and slipped through it.

That someone was Jasmine.

What the hell was she up to? If she'd stolen the scroll, he had to get it back. If he didn't, the museum would hold Hank's team responsible for the theft, especially considering they were the security team.

The copper scroll was a national treasure. If he didn't get it back, it could cause an international incident as well as delay film production.

Ace slipped out of the museum and paused to locate the thief.

Dark hair flashed as Jasmine rounded the corner of a building across the street from the museum.

Ace had to wait for a delivery truck to pass in front of him before he could cross the road. As he waited, two large men dressed in black entered the side street, heading in the same direction as Jasmine.

Once the delivery truck passed, Ace crossed the street and broke into a jog, hurrying toward the street Jasmine had turned onto.

As Ace reached the corner of the building, he heard a woman shout, "No!"

He turned onto the street.

A block away, the two men in black had Jasmine by her arms. She fought like a wildcat, kicking, twisting, and struggling while holding onto the satchel looped over her neck and shoulder. One man ripped the scarf from her head and reached for the satchel's strap.

"Hey!" Ace yelled, racing toward the men.

Jasmine used the distraction to twist and kick the man on her right in the groin. When he doubled over, she brought her knee up, slamming it into his face.

The injured man released her arm.

Jasmine turned to the other man, but not soon enough. He backhanded her on the side of her face hard enough to send her flying.

As she fell backward, the man grabbed the satchel and yanked, pulling it over her head as she fell hard against the wall of a building.

Clutching the satchel like a football, the man ran. His partner staggered to his feet and followed.

Ace would have gone after them but was more concerned about Jasmine.

The men ran to the end of the street. A car pulled up, they dove in, and, in seconds, they were gone.

Jasmine lay against the wall, her eyes closed, a red mark on her cheek where the man had hit her.

Anger burned in Ace's gut. He wanted to go after the men and beat the shit out of them. But he couldn't leave this injured woman lying in the street.

He knelt beside her and touched her shoulder. "Jasmine."

Jasmine moaned, blinked her eyes open and stared up into his face, her brow furrowing. "Ace?

What—" She glanced around, her frown deepening. "Where am I?" She met his gaze again. "Is it really you?"

His lips turned up on the corners. "Yes, it's me. You're in Jordan." His brow dipped. "You were attacked."

She pinched the bridge of her nose. "What happened?"

"Two men attacked you," he said.

"Two men..." She shook her head slowly. "Jordan..." Then her eyes widened, and she looked around frantically. "My satchel! Where is my satchel?"

"The men who hurt you took it."

She struggled to get to her feet. "Where did they go? I have to get it back." As she stood, she swayed.

Ace slipped an arm around her narrow waist. "They're gone."

"No!" She raked a hand through her hair. "I need that satchel." Jasmine pushed away from Ace and started running back the way they'd come, then stopped and looked over her shoulder. "Which way did they go?"

He tipped his head in the direction the men had gone.

When Jasmine turned in that direction, Ace stepped in front of her and gripped her arms. "They're gone. You won't catch up to them now."

"Why didn't you stop them? They stole my satchel!" She tried to shake off his grip on her arms.

His lips pressed together, and his grip tightened. "What was in the satchel, Jasmine?"

"Something important. I have to get it back. Please, let go of me."

"Was the copper scroll in your bag?" he asked quietly so only she could hear his words.

Her gaze locked with his. For a moment, she hesitated, as if deciding whether or not to trust him. Then she nodded. "I had to take it. If I don't get it back, someone I care about will die."

Thank you for reading EMI'S HERO and the first chapter of ATHENS AFFAIR.

If you want to read more about Athens Affair click Here

# ABOUT THE AUTHOR

ELLE JAMES also writing as MYLA JACKSON is a *New York Times* and *USA Today* Bestselling author of books including cowboys, intrigues and paranormal adventures that keep her readers on the edges of their seats. When she's not at her computer, she's traveling, snow skiing, boating, or riding her ATV, dreaming up new stories. Learn more about Elle James at www.ellejames.com

Website | Facebook | Twitter | GoodReads | Newsletter | BookBub | Amazon

Or visit her alter ego Myla Jackson at mylajackson.com
Website | Facebook | Twitter | Newsletter

*Follow Me!*
www.ellejames.com
ellejamesauthor@gmail.com

# ALSO BY ELLE JAMES

Fool's Folly (#9)

Colorado Free Rein (#10)

Rocky Mountain Venom (#11)

High Country Hero (#12)

### *Brotherhood Protectors*

Montana SEAL (#1)

Bride Protector SEAL (#2)

Montana D-Force (#3)

Cowboy D-Force (#4)

Montana Ranger (#5)

Montana Dog Soldier (#6)

Montana SEAL Daddy (#7)

Montana Ranger's Wedding Vow (#8)

Montana SEAL Undercover Daddy (#9)

Cape Cod SEAL Rescue (#10)

Montana SEAL Friendly Fire (#11)

Montana SEAL's Mail-Order Bride (#12)

SEAL Justice (#13)

Ranger Creed (#14)

Delta Force Rescue (#15)

Dog Days of Christmas (#16)

Montana Rescue (#17)

Montana Ranger Returns (#18)

Brotherhood Protectors Boxed Set 1

Brotherhood Protectors Boxed Set 2

Brotherhood Protectors Boxed Set 3

Brotherhood Protectors Boxed Set 4

Brotherhood Protectors Boxed Set 5

Brotherhood Protectors Boxed Set 6

### *Iron Horse Legacy*

Soldier's Duty (#1)

Ranger's Baby (#2)

Marine's Promise (#3)

SEAL's Vow (#4)

Warrior's Resolve (#5)

Drake (#6)

Grimm (#7)

Murdock (#8)

Utah (#9)

Judge (#10)

### *Delta Force Strong*

Ivy's Delta (Delta Force 3 Crossover)

Breaking Silence (#1)

Breaking Rules (#2)

Breaking Away (#3)

Breaking Free (#4)

Breaking Hearts (#5)

Engaged with the Boss

Cowboy Brigade

An Unexpected Clue

Under Suspicion, With Child

Texas-Size Secrets

Made in United States
Cleveland, OH
22 April 2025

16323807R00181